MEN OF SIEGE BOOK FOUR

FALCON

BEX DANE

Falcon (Men of Siege Book Four) © 2019 by Bex Dane.

Published by Larken Romance

First Edition 2019

Cover by Elizabeth Mackey Designs

Falcon (Men of Siege Book Four)

The battle royale that ends with a big climax.

Aida

I want Falcon to make me moan.

Yes, he's a cold-hearted killer who cares about no one but himself.

And he's holding me hostage, forcing me to admit my life is a lie, before he gives me what I want.

He'll tease me till I beg but always stops before I reach the edge.

But he underestimates the woman I've become.

He still thinks of me as the lost child he rescued years ago.

I'm all grown up now and I have my own weapons to use in our war.

Falcon

Aida's testing all my limits.

Playing bodyguard to an opera diva is not my kind of mission.

I'd rather be out systematically dismantling my father's drug cartel.

But Aida's being targeted by a sophisticated enemy.

She needs me to keep her safe.

Oh, I'll make her moan. No doubt.

Rest assured, she'll give me her secrets first.

She may bring me to my knees, but I never lose.

Falcon is a standalone novel in the Men of Siege series. If you like opposites-attract, second-chance romance, you'll love Falcon.

Become a VIP

———————

SIGN UP TO BEX DANE's VIP reader team and receive exclusive bonus content including;

- Free books

- Advanced Reader Copies

- Behind-the-scenes secrets no one else knows

Get all this by signing up at bexdane[1].com[2]

---

1. https://bexdane.com/

2. https://bexdane.com/

Chapter 1

NUEVO LAREDO, MEXICO

Twenty-two years ago

Primitivo (Falcon)

"Everyone out. Run!"

Startled eyes stared back at me.

The group of women in the brothel parlor didn't move. They had no idea they were sitting ducks before a massacre.

"Oscar's about to burst through that door and start shooting."

One of the women snapped out of it and ran.

"Get the fuck up and run!" I yelled at the rest of them.

Finally, they screamed and followed her.

"Claudia!" My call died in the chaos.

Shit, I should've located her first before sounding the alarm, but I panicked when Oscar left early. Weeks of planning and I fucked it up.

I slammed the butt of my rifle into the first bedroom door. "Get up. Now. Shooter at the front. Go out the back. Hurry. Hurry!"

Women dressed in miniskirts and underwear bumped in the narrow hallway, gasping in their frantic rush.

They raced without looking back. They ran for their lives.

"Claudia!"

No one answered me.

Where the hell was she? I found her daughter crouched in the hallway with her hands over her ears.

"Where's your mom?"

Magdalena's round, terrified eyes peered up at me. "She's gone."

"Gone? Where?"

"I..."

Fuck. We didn't have time to talk. "Get out. Wait by my truck. Go now!"

She scurried out the back just as my brother broke through the front door. He squeezed his eyes shut and opened fire. The bastard didn't even see me.

I took cover behind the couch with my rifle over the top as his wild shots blasted through the room. My heart racing, I took aim and shot him in the thigh.

He stopped shooting but didn't go down. "What the hell?"

"Drop your weapon, Oscar."

He opened his eyes and scanned the empty room.

In his cocaine haze, he didn't feel pain from the bullet in his leg.

"Drop the rifle, Oscar," I repeated.

His wild eyes zeroed in on me. "You shoot me, not them?" Spit came from his scowling mouth as he spoke.

I held my fire. I always protected my brothers. As the oldest son, the responsibility fell on me. I risked my life to save theirs many times. But when it came to killing women, I drew the line. I had to stop him, brotherly fidelity be damned.

"They did nothing to harm us." I tilted my head toward the back door.

Manuel, the leader of a rival gang, had brutally murdered the whores in my father's brothel last week. Fifteen dead. My father ordered this attack as retribution.

His eyes glanced to the door and back to me. "They killed ours, we kill theirs." Oscar rattled off the mantra my father had drilled into our heads since infancy.

"No. We don't kill innocent women over this turf war."

"We kill whoever we need to." He narrowed his gaze and trained his rifle on me.

"I don't want to shoot you, Oscar." I gave him his final warning.

"You betray the family?" His voice rasped with rage.

Yes. The ultimate betrayal of my family and our history. "You can't betray evil, only escape it."

His weapon shook as he pressed the trigger. He'd forced my hand. It was him or me.

I shot Oscar in the chest.

He gasped and fell. Thank God my mama wasn't alive to see me spill my own brother's blood. I grabbed his rifle and didn't spare a second to say goodbye. The survivors must carry on or become the dead.

At the back of the house, Magdalena stood crying on the passenger side of my truck.

Just a tiny thing, I towered over her. "Claudia's not here?"

"Manuel took her before you got here." Tears streaked through the dirt on her face. "She said she'd be back. She didn't know when." Her hair fell forward as she sobbed into her hands.

Goddammit. Manuel got to Claudia. I missed her by minutes. I should've planned this better. Of course Manuel would hear about the attack and run with Claudia, the one woman my father would want.

This left her daughter alone.

With me.

"Get in." I opened the door and shoved her inside.

After running around the front, I tossed the two rifles on the seat and started up the truck.

"We're leaving without her?" her timid voice asked me.

"We have no choice." A boat waited for us in the Gulf. We needed to be on it before my father realized someone had transferred his millions to offshore accounts.

Dust kicked up around us as the tires skidded in the dirt. She sat up and peered out the windshield as Nuevo Laredo faded in the distance.

Adios, Papá.

Chapter 2

WHEN SOLEDAD OPENED the door to her apartment in Madison, New Jersey, it took a moment before her eyes flashed with recognition. Her mouth drew taut like she'd seen a ghost. Females often reacted with fear when I showed up. Primitivo de la Cruz on your doorstep rarely meant good news.

"Let us in."

She backed up to let us enter, but still eyed me cautiously.

"You're safe with me, Soledad. You know that. I need your help."

"Sure, Tivo. Whatever you need. I mean I owe you so much." She spoke quickly.

"You don't owe me anything. You helped me too. The route worked for us just as it did for you." A year ago she had bravely tested the escape route for me. She took a hired boat ride across the Gulf of Mexico to Texas where she borrowed a car to trek across the country, finally landing in New Jersey. Magdalena and I had done the same and made it safely.

Her shoulders relaxed and her big brown eyes crinkled with her smile. She had a long oval face framed by shiny straight sable hair. She was thin and tall, pert breasts, the body of a dancer.

"What's with the child?" she asked.

Magdalena curled her shoulders down and hid behind me. We hadn't talked to anyone but each other for a week. She'd been shy at first, but slowly opened up and started talking. I'd discovered she was crazy about lasagna and she liked to sing. She'd asked about her mom, and I'd promised her I would find her. Truth was, finding Manuel and Claudia would be a challenge, but I couldn't tell her that. She was too upset.

"She's clearly not a child." Magdalena had long legs, full round breasts, and a curvy ass. Pretty like her mother. More than once I caught her watching me dress, and more than once I was tempted to kiss her. But she was only fifteen, scared, and alone. Didn't ask her if she was a virgin, but either way, the last thing she needed was to kiss a gangster like me.

"Who is she?" Soledad repeated her question.

"She's Claudia's daughter."

Soledad stepped back and stared at Magdalena like she had leprosy.

Magdalena flinched and lowered her head.

My words lay heavy in the air. I'd informed Soledad of the heated quarrel between Manuel and my father over Claudia. Soledad had once been in the same position. She'd encouraged me to get Claudia away from the situation quickly.

Soledad took a deep breath and offered Magdalena a gentle smile. "What's your name, sweetheart?" She bent down to meet Magdalena's eyes.

"Magdalena." The vulnerability coming off the girl had to touch Soledad. Shoot. I felt it and I was a soulless killer.

Soledad looked up at me again. "Where is Claudia?" The stress in her voice told me she already had a good idea what had happened.

"My father ordered me to kill all of Manuel's girls but spare Claudia and her daughter. He wanted me to bring them to him."

"But you didn't?"

"No. I'd planned to help them escape. Manuel left with Claudia before I could get her out. I'm going to find her and bring her back. I need you to watch the girl for me."

Her brow scrunched. "How old is she?"

"Fifteen." Magdalena spoke for herself.

"Fifteen," Soledad repeated slowly and quietly. Her mind must be doing the math. If I didn't find her mother, Soledad would be taking her on for at least three years.

"Manuel had a quinceañera planned for her. We both know she's better off here."

All the girls who had a quinceañera were forced to prostitute like Claudia. I'd saved her just in time. Soledad knew this because she had been forced into prostitution at fifteen too. Not by Manuel, by my father.

"I can't take her." She looked down at her feet.

"Why not?" Soledad never said no to me. My disappointment with her response rang in my angry voice.

When she looked up, her eyes pleaded with me. "I'm leaving for New York. I'm enrolled at an art school. I have to pack. I'll be busy. She needs schooling and ID and many things I have no idea how to give her."

This was news to me. "Art school? Dance?'

"Yes." She grinned a shy smile.

A surge of pride passed through me. Soledad came alone to New Jersey, seized the opportunity, and was making a life for herself.

"You take her with you to New York. Enroll her in school too. She can sing."

Magdalena's head popped up.

"Sing the paloma song, Magdalena." Under the stars on a boat in the Gulf, she sang a sad song about a dove. She sang like an angel. A morbid, morose angel, but still talented.

"No, Tivo. Don't ask me to do that."

I turned my frown from her to Soledad. "Get her into high school in the same city, then get her into your art school."

Soledad shook her head. "I can't take Claudia's daughter with me to New York. It puts me right in the middle between Manuel and your father. I'll open my door one day and find a gun at my head. I can't risk it."

She stated the truth. There were huge risks here. "It's just temporary until I find Claudia and get her away from Manuel."

"I don't know."

I stepped closer to Soledad, and she sucked in a sharp breath. Not fear this time, attraction. She was eight years older than me, but we'd had sex a few times. Really good sex. Didn't mean anything. I was just showing her how good it could be after the misery she'd experienced under my father's rule. Pure physical pleasure. For both of us. I leaned down with my lips close to her ear. "It's late. Set Magdalena up on the couch."

Her questioning eyes looked into mine, and I gave her a slight nod.

"Okay." She said with a breathy smile and a bit of surrender.

Chapter 3

MAGDALENA

I came out of the shower and didn't see Tivo or his friend Soledad.

Relief rushed through me at not having to face them again. That whole conversation was so humiliating. My mother had become a pawn in a stupid turf war between two vicious gangs, and I was trouble by association.

Muted noises came from Soledad's closed bedroom door. Soft moans. Oh no. Was he hurting her? No. Tivo looked mean and carried lots of guns, but he wouldn't hurt a woman. Would he?

A blanket and sheet awaited me on the couch, so I unfolded them and tucked them in around the edges. The sheets felt soft on my skin. I loved the colors. Stripes in shades of purple that blended like a piece of art. Soledad lived in a nice place. Vibrant green plants in the corners looked happy and well maintained. She said Tivo had helped her. There were no signs she was unhappy or anything could be going wrong in the room.

I lay down and listened some more. The moans grew louder. Furniture creaked. Her bed? Rhythmic grunts joined the moans. Oh goodness. He wasn't hurting her. She was experiencing pleasure. Great pleasure. Like nothing I'd ever heard!

What could a man do to a woman to make them moan in pleasure like that? Were they having sex? My mom never moaned when she had sex with the johns at Manuel's brothel. Soledad clearly enjoyed intercourse. It sounded like Tivo was having fun too. The grunts and groans built to a crescendo and obvious climax. I bit my lip to keep my mouth from gaping open. Harsh breaths, some rustling, and Tivo's deep voice murmuring followed. Then silence.

I felt like crying. I'd spent a week crushing on Tivo and he never so much as held my hand. We'd been with Soledad only a few hours and he'd already had sex with her. Why didn't he want me?

I closed my eyes and pretended to sleep, but uncertainty and excitement danced and pinged around my head. My world felt rocked. My life of violence, drugs, and poverty faded in the distance. In the future, I spied a world with schools for girls who could sing where women could enjoy sex so much they moaned. A new world with luxuriously soft sheets.

I missed my mother and worried about her, but I trusted Tivo to find her. I already thought Tivo hung the sun and the moon, but now I knew. He was a superhero.

―――――――――

I LAY QUIETLY ON THE couch, trying to catch my breath after all the excitement of this week. Tivo opened the door to Soledad's room. His normally slicked back hair flopped forward as he looked down to button his baggy jeans. He fastened the top button only of a plaid shirt he wore over a white tank top.

Of all Guillermo's sons, I found Tivo the most handsome. He had the longest lashes, the broadest shoulders, and an undeniable confidence the girls back home swooned over.

He bent down in front of me, resting his elbows on his knees. His eyes were light blue. Rare among the men of our town and unlike his father who had evil dark eyes. Maybe Tivo was the light to his darkness.

Tivo didn't appear to be happy like he should after just having great sex. He looked sad and drained.

"I'm leaving." His voice came out barely a whisper.

Leaving? A stone as heavy as a boulder dropped in my stomach. Tivo was all I had. I'd become attached to him.

"Please don't leave me, Tivo."

He shook his head. "You'll stay here with Soledad. She'll help you." He looked down at the floor. "I'll find your mother."

"I want that more than anything, but I don't want you to leave me to do it."

"I have to go. No one else can find her but me."

"I'm scared." A new country, a big city, a stranger's apartment. Everything felt unfamiliar and terrifying.

"I know. Be brave. Okay? Be like Soledad. She's doing well. She'll be a role model for you."

My eyes stung. I hiccuped, trying to hold it in, but I couldn't. I'd be all alone without Tivo. The tears fell and dropped onto my lap.

He looked up and examined my face. His hand came up slowly. The back of his index finger brushed a tear from the apple of my cheek.

"No crying." His pretty blue eyes went soft. "Don't cry. Sing."

I blinked a few times, not understanding him. "What?"

"Sing loud and strong and from your heart. Take all these tears and turn them into song. It's the way it should be. You should sing and cry and laugh. All the things a woman does in her life."

He wanted me to sing. Why? "And moan?" I don't know why I asked him that. His eyebrows curled high on his forehead.

"Repeat that, please."

"When I become a woman, should I moan? Like Soledad, my role model?"

He stood up and paced away from me. His hands gripped the long hair on the top of his head and tugged. He turned and pinned me with his light eyes. "You heard us?"

I looked down, feeling terrible after accusing him like that. "You made her moan."

He took three quick strides back to me and grasped my cheeks in his palms. "Yes, alright, mi paloma?"

My dove. He'd given me the endearment on the boat here after I sang a Mexican folk song called "Cucurrucucu Paloma." I thought I'd heard him wrong, but he did it again. He called me his dove. Had Tivo grown to care for me as I had him?

"I want you to fucking moan. You find a man that makes you moan like that or you kick him out of your bed. You understand?"

I held my breath, waiting for him to go on or let go, but he didn't. He wanted me to respond. "Yes," I managed to get out. "My mom never..."

"Your mom had it bad. Manual and my father used her up. The entire neighborhood used her. She was forced to have sex with twenty different men each night or Manuel would beat her. She was forced to sleep with my father or he would kill her. I guarantee you she didn't enjoy one second of that. I wanted to help her. I tried so hard. Manuel got to her first. I'll do my best to get her back for you, but until then you sing for her. Moan and laugh and sing for her. All the gifts she never had. She will live them through you as her spirit is in you." His forehead pressed to mine, and his hands moved to squeeze the back of my neck. "She would want you to sing. Understand me?" He had never talked to me like that before, emotional and caring. But what was he saying?

He wanted me to sing for my mom. For her memory. My heart squeezed. "Yes." I placed my hands on his strong forearms, and we froze like that in our half-way hug. "I'll do what you say, but she's not dead. Manuel won't kill her. He loves her."

He pulled away and the warmth from his hands left my cheeks. "My father loves her too, and Manuel will use her to get his revenge."

True. My mom was in great danger. "You have to find her before he kills her."

"I will. And I promise you Manuel and my father will pay for this. I'll slaughter every one of their soldiers first and them last."

He'd spend his life getting revenge? Revenge led to nothing. I'd seen too much of it growing up in the brothels. "That's no way to live. You need to sing and cry and moan too."

His eyes cooled and shut down. Our talk was over. He stood and walked toward Soledad's kitchen. "I don't sing."

Chapter 4

———

BOSTON, MASSACHUSETTS

Present day

Falcon (Primitivo)

Decked out dinner tables ran from the kitchen to the living room of Rogan's ranch house. Tessa pranced around with her sweet-as-sin smile and a skin-tight sweater dress. She rocked the high-heeled boots up to her knees. She had her hair up in a bun on top of her head tied with a big red bow. Cute and sexy. She clapped her hands. "Take a seat, everyone. Dinner is ready."

Tessa invited every Tom, Dick, and Harry to Christmas dinner. Even the cowboy from the trial was here, Zook. His wife, Cecelia, had her hair pulled back tight like a librarian. How the hell did he get a classy chick like her to marry his ex-con ass?

At Tessa's request, for the holidays, Rogan, Dallas, and Brock all set aside their differences with FBI Secret Agent Lachlan Cutlass. Lachlan brought a spitfire redhead. Bet she was wild in the sheets. A new kid named Jeremy followed Tessa around like a puppy, eager to help her set plates and light candles.

Torrez and Soraya showed up too. She still dressed fine and freaky like she did before she married the ass. All the hot chicks here were taken, and none of these dudes shared. Seemed selfish to me. They found a bitch who puts out, they should share with the single brothers. I was pretty sure Soraya would be open to it if Torrez would get the possessive rod out of his ass and let me fuck his wife.

Tori came with Cyan this year. Now Tori didn't have a rock on her left ring finger. I could fuck her. That would liven up this party. Nah, Tori was a nice girl. She'd get all mushy are-you-gonna-call-me after. No way in hell I'd call her for a second round. She was exactly the reason I didn't fuck single chicks. I had this thought every time I saw Tori. She needed to get married so I could fuck her.

All Tessa's sisters, their husbands, and their kids hustled over to the table. The rest of Z Security—Ruger, Oz, Diesel, and Blaze—stayed in their seats. They looked as uncomfortable and unenthusiastic as me.

The collar of this shirt cut off my air supply. Somebody get my gun. I'd rather blow my own head off than sit here watching shiny happy people smile and exchange sparkly crap.

Such a waste of time. We could be working out, chasing bad guys, planning murders, but no, we all had to sit around and pretend to be normal.

Rogan walked toward me in the living room, away from the table he'd been instructed to sit at. "You comin' to sit down for my speech?"

I loathed his emo state of the union address, and Rogan loved to rub it in my face.

"Was about to go have a smoke." I kept my eyes on Soraya.

"You taking up smoking?" The laugh in his voice made me crack a grin.

"Thinkin' about it."

Tessa came up to us, and he stood a little taller when she got in his space. "We're ready. I asked you guys to have a seat."

"Bring the food out first, Tess." Rogan wrapped an arm behind her back and pulled her close.

She looked up at him. "No, Rogan. It'll get cold. You do the speech first, and then I'll bring it out."

Rogan stared at her for a second. "Alright." Man, he was so whipped. She could ask him anything and he'd say alright.

She grinned and turned to me. "Milo wants to sit next to the man with wings." Her pretty green eyes flirted with me.

Damn. I couldn't turn her down either. "Right." I stood and made my way to the empty seat Milo had saved for me.

"You sit right here, Falcon."

Unlike most kids, who usually ran from me, Milo had some weird interest in the obscure. Maybe he was trying to replace his father, Jeb Barebones, who was writing his manifesto from federal prison. But Milo shouldn't look to me for anything. I had nothing to offer him unless he wanted to grow up to be a screwed up in the head hitman too.

Everyone settled in their seats, and Rogan stood at the head of the table. As he blew his mouth off about family and shit, I let my mind wander through the other Christmases we'd spent together. At least five in Afghanistan or Syria, nothing to eat but MREs. The Christmas after Eden died, we blasted mud pits with RPGs. Now that was quality family time.

Tessa and the last three years had changed Rogan. He made his decisions with her in mind. He overdid the effort to minimize potential risks to us in the line of duty. Working for him was boring as hell, but he still hit the shooting range weekly with me, he made physical training a priority, and he kept his tactical skills sharp.

"Now let's eat." He bent down and kissed Tessa and everyone raised their glasses to clink them together.

Milo lifted his milk cup toward me. I stared at it, grabbed my whiskey, and tapped his cup. "Merry Christmas, kid."

He smiled big as Tessa and Jeremy carried out dish after dish to pass around. We all loaded our plates with a shit ton of calories. I passed on most of it, except Tessa's spoonbread. That stuff tasted so good, it was worth the three extra hours at the gym to work it off.

No one but me noticed Rogan dropping his fork to check his phone. His gaze slid to mine.

I'd seen that look many times through the years. Shit was going down. Hopefully some good shit. Tessa stopped talking to her sister to look at Rogan.

"Just a second." He stood and walked to the kitchen. Tessa and I followed him.

He leaned against the counter and pressed his phone to his ear. "How many shooters?" he asked.

Cool. A shooting. I'm up for that.

"How many dead?" Rogan looked at me again. "We'll be there by morning. Tell the airport and Bastien. No one else." Bastien was his stepdad and the prime minister of a small Caribbean island. Rogan ended the call. "Shooting on St. Amalie. Six dead. Two shooters, assassination style."

Tessa gasped. "Oh no."

"They get 'em?" I asked. Shooters often kill themselves or get shot before they escape.

"No. They got away by boat. Security on the island sucks. I've been hounding Bastien about it since we heard Soraya was kidnapped from there. He feels overwhelmed. He wants to bring us in to help with the investigation and advise on a security taskforce."

"Cool. A little island vacation." I rubbed my hands together and smiled.

Rogan glared at me. Tessa's mouth dropped open.

"Of course this is very serious." Rogan and Tessa saw right through my fake solemnity, but they didn't care. They had to face this news and what it meant; they had to separate.

My muscles tensed, bracing for the deluge of sentimental crap. Did someone leave the oven open? Because this kitchen suddenly felt very hot.

I tried to sneak out before the tears started, but Rogan stopped me. "Stand by, Falc. We need to prep."

I lingered by the door and turned my back on them.

"Sorry about dinner," Rogan said to her.

Oh yeah, her dinner was ruined too. Sucked for Tessa, good news for me.

"You're leaving?" She sounded sad but resigned.

"Yeah, babe."

She didn't bother asking if she could come with us. Since Eden died because she followed Rogan, he never allowed Tessa near any action.

"Just be careful."

"I'll be back and running to you as soon as my feet hit the ground."

Someone kill me before I barf. Fuck, she turned Rogan into a giant ball of cheese with almonds mashed into it.

The kitchen door opened and a stream of men filed in. They must've sensed the tension when Rogan, Tessa, and I left the table.

Ruger, Oz, Lachlan, Diesel, Blaze, Dallas, Brock, Torrez, and Zook stared at Rogan.

"There's been a shooting on St. Amalie. Six dead. Falcon and I are heading out to investigate."

"The FBI should be on that," Lachlan said.

Rogan shook his head. "Out of their jurisdiction."

"Who are you taking?" Dallas asked Rogan.

"I'll take Alpha Squadron. Ruger, Oz, Diesel, Blaze, and Falcon."

Nice. Alpha Squadron as a unit again. Wouldn't be as much action as Delta Force, but we'd find some trouble for sure.

There was some grumbling because everyone wanted to go.

"If things heat up, I'll call the rest of you. Now go back and finish your dinner."

"If you need anything, just call," Brock said to Rogan, implying if he needed to order a hit, Brock would take the heat for him.

"No thanks, buddy." Rogan refused. He didn't do anything illegal. Like I said, boring as hell, but consistent, stable, and loyal.

Excelente.

This holiday just got unfucked.

Chapter 5

—————

ST. AMALIE, THE CARIBBEAN

"You can go. We'll contact you if we need anything." I sat back and waited for the couple I just finished questioning to get up and leave.

They'd checked out squeaky clean. No possible ties to the shooting. The wife, who had started the interview staring at me like I was about to rape her, changed her demeanor to assessing eyes, traveling over my arms and inspecting my tattoos. She blushed when I caught her looking.

"C'mon, Iris." Her husband tugged her arm and pulled her away.

Relax, Freddie. Wouldn't fuck her anyway. Too skinny.

Rogan walked over to me from the station where he'd conducted his interviews.

"We done?" I had enough people for today. All this pretending to care drained me to no end.

"One more couple. They want us to come up to the penthouse suite." He quirked his lips.

"They're too good to come down to the ballroom to be interviewed?" Seemed odd for a witness to make demands of the investigators.

"Possible red flag," he said.

"Not possible. Obvious red flag."

We took the elevator to the fifteenth floor of the resort in St. Amalie. Rogan knocked on the door.

A man opened it. About five-foot-ten. Wearing slacks and a business shirt with a jacket. Overdressed for the casual island. He had milky white skin, long fingers and legs, and held himself tall as he looked down his nose at us.

"Come in." He spoke with a Euro accent. Couldn't place it.

He moved aside to let us into a huge pad with panoramic views of the crystal blue ocean. We were above the tops of the palm trees up here. Swank. Posh. Snobby.

Rogan scanned the room, his gaze stopping on a table and chairs near the window. "Can I talk to you over there?"

"But of course."

That accent. French or Italian.

"Are there two of you?" I asked him.

"Yes, my wife is in the bedroom." He lowered his chin and focused his eyes on me. Very dramatic. "Please be gentle with her."

"Sure." No fucking way. She'd made us come up to her suite, now she was hiding in her bedroom, she wasn't getting kid-glove treatment. Gentle was not in my repertoire.

I passed through the open bedroom door without knocking. She sat on a lounge by the window, hot pink high-heeled sandals crossed at the ankle. She wore a flowing silk dress, the huge slit up the side showing her exposed legs. The dress looked like Picasso barfed geometric shapes on it. Big Bird yellow, Miss Piggy pink, and Kermit green. A black rope criss-crossed over her torso and hung down her left thigh, tassels swaying at the end.

Shiny black shades with diamonds along the sides covered half of her face. Brunette bangs concealed the rest of it. All she had showing was her painted red lips, the tip of her nose, and her chin. She had one arm propped up on the back of the chaise lounge, the other hanging loose by her side. A despondent Cleopatra. Give me a fucking break.

When her peripheral vision caught sight of me, she gasped and sat up.

She pulled her legs up to her chest. The dress opened up to show part of her ample ass. Nice.

"I need to ask you some questions."

She stared at me for a long time. Too long. Her head tilted and her forehead wrinkles dipped behind her glasses. What was her fucking problem?

She shook her head, brushing off whatever the hell she was thinking, and stood up. She turned toward the window with her long, velvet hair trailing down her back. The bottom of her dress rubbed the carpet like a wedding veil. "What are you doing here?" Her voice held a harsh rasp. What was with all the drama?

"Your husband just sent me in here to ask you some questions."

"So ask," she said without looking at me.

"Alright. What's your name?"

You'd think that would be a simple question. Not for this one. She pivoted and stared at me through her glasses, crossed her arms over her chest, and leaned toward me. "You don't know who I am?"

She blew out a long breath. Frustrated as hell with me. All I did was ask her name. What a fucking diva.

I didn't keep up on pop culture. I had better shit to do, like stalking and killing people. "Not a clue. Are you some kind of reality TV star, and I'm supposed to know who you are?"

Her lips pouted and she leaned back to stand up straight again. "Are you some kind of buffed-up goon asking me stupid questions?"

She spoke with a Euro accent too. Not very strong. Affected, like she was controlling it. There's no way she was French too. Her skin was too dark. Unless she'd been here a long time and had a great tan, I'd guess she was Italian or Spanish. Or Mexican. Her spitfire attitude sure reminded me of my mom before she passed. "Asking a witness her name is not a stupid question. It's a basic question that is taking too fucking long for you to answer."

She pulled her arms tighter to her chest, pushing up a nice sets of boobs in a black bikini top. "Actually, I'm a housewife."

When she smiled, I noticed fang-like incisors protruding beyond her front teeth. An imperfection in a woman putting out a lot of effort to look perfect.

"That would be good to know if I had asked what you do, but I didn't. I asked you what's your name." My ass she was a housewife. This woman had never cleaned a commode in her life.

"I am Aida Soltari." She said each syllable with emphasis.

Eye-ee-da Sol-tar-ee

She definitely expected me to recognize the name. Sorry, lady.

"Okay, Mrs. Soltari, tell me what you saw yesterday."

She waltzed back to her lounge and sat down as she spoke. "Well... I saw Mount Pintaro. I saw a toucan."

What the hell was her game? "Did you see six women get shot on the dock of this resort?"

She tilted her head to the side. "No," she said curtly.

"No?"

"I didn't see anything."

"Did you hear there was a shooting yesterday?"

"No, I haven't heard about it."

Okay, this just went from weird to crazy town. Most women quivered in front of me, and this one gave me complete attitude. For a brief second, I imagined smacking her ass on the bed and teaching her a lesson or two about buffed-up goons and lying during a murder investigation. She met all my criteria for a fuck. Married, big tits and ass, high heels. Totally fuckable. Too bad she was a smart-mouthed reality show has-been.

She raised a curled finger to her nose and sniffed.

Cue the tears, Freddie.

"Six young women were killed on the dock of this resort yesterday. Shot execution style. And you didn't hear about it?"

"Nope." Her lips quivered and an honest-to-God tear dripped out under the rim of her glasses. She took them off to wipe her eye with the back of her index finger.

Holy shit.

Had I fucked his woman? I would remember those tits. No. I hadn't fucked her. Then why did her tears make me want to run? Because any tears made me want to run, but hers... sparked something inside me. Not compassion, but remorse. Like I should apologize to her.

"Look out your window, Mrs. Soltari." My voice softened for some reason. "You see crime scene tape down at the dock? You see blood stains on the wood?" I stepped closer and looked down. Yep, still there. She couldn't deny it.

She turned her head away. "No. They're not dead." She whimpered and put her glasses back on.

And there it was again. A tapping at my gut like the spear of a toothpick. I knew this woman. Maybe I'd seen her on TV and didn't remember her. Maybe I had screwed her and broke her heart.

Either way, fuck this noise. I'm outta here. "We'll contact you if we need more info." We definitely needed more info, but Rogan would have to be the one to crack this nutcase.

I turned my back on her and walked out. I don't do lying, crying bitches.

"Adios, Aida."

I marched out the door without a word to Rogan or the diva's stupid husband.

———

IN THE HALLWAY, I SLAMMED open a side door leading to a balcony. The sea air hit me and I sucked it in. Anger roiled up in my stomach. What the hell just happened?

What was it about her? I tamped it down with one breath. Anger was a wasted emotion that clouded the judgment. I needed to think clearly.

The toothpick poke in my gut had grown to the size of a skewer and moved up to my heart. A tiny boat braving the waters of the Gulf Coast. A road trip through the South and up the East Coast. A young girl who sang like an angel.

A promise to a girl that I would find her mother.

A promise I had failed to keep.

Magdalena. The girl I'd disappointed.

Not sure what I was doing, I pulled up my phone and dialed a number I hadn't called in twenty-two years.

No answer.

Fuck. I leaned my arms on the rails of the balcony and tried again to stuff down the emotions. They only sucked you dry and killed.

I googled her name. Jesus. Red carpets. Outdoor arenas. Rubbing shoulders with people so famous even I had heard of them. Gaspar Evaristo. My mother loved him. Pictures of her on the stage wearing heavy makeup and a green dress. She sat on her knees crying before a man dressed like a viking whose mouth was open as he sang. A Latina Choice nomination for a pop song...

A call came through on my phone. Soledad. Calling me back.

"Hello."

"Primitivo?"

No one had called me that in a long time. The skewer in my heart poked out a gaping hole.

"Yes." Despite everything, I was still Primitivo.

"Did you call me?"

My heart raced. Shut that shit down, Falcon. "What became of Magdalena?" I couldn't keep the intensity from my voice.

"I... You never asked. All this time."

I didn't ask. I didn't want to know. "I'm asking now. What became of Magdalena?" My voice stung with urgency.

She whimpered. "She's a singer."

"What name does she go by?"

"She wouldn't want me to tell you. She's put her past behind her."

"What name does she go by?"

"Why do you need to know?"

"Why? Because I'm on an island called St. Amalie where six women were executed on the dock. I got a crazy bitch who won't answer any questions, and my gut is telling me to call you. So you wanna tell me what name she goes by so I can sort this out?"

After a heavy sigh, she said, "She is known as Aida Soltari."

Goddamn Magdalena lied to me. Sat right in front of me and lied through her teeth.

"Is she okay?" I barely heard Soledad's question. My mind was racing.

"Yeah. I saw her. She's okay."

"Please protect her, Tivo."

"Why do you say that?"

"There was a bomb at her last concert in Zurich. She went to St. Amalie to recover from the stress. And now there's been a shooting. I'm worried about her. She's fragile. She'll need support."

Again with the fragile crap. "She has a husband."

"He can't protect her. Not like you can. I don't trust Thorne anyway. Something shady about him."

I thought the same of the French guy. "Alright. I'll see what I can do."

I slammed the balcony door open and stormed right back to her room. I banged hard on her door. Rogan opened it. I pushed through and charged to her room.

She had returned to her chaise lounge and wasn't wearing the glasses anymore. Looking at her now, I saw it. She had Magdalena's wide eyes, too big for her face, the petite nose, round cheeks and the square chin I remembered.

"You lied to me."

She gasped and put her hands to her chest. "Get out!"

"You fucking lied to me."

"I did not," she retorted.

"You are not Aida Soltari."

"I most certainly am." Her hands balled into fists.

"You are Magdalena Esperanza." I said it mean and harsh. I supposed I should've been "gentle" like they told me, but she pissed me off with her bullshit.

Her head jerked back. "I am not."

"You lie. You lie as the day is long."

"Get out." She stood up and pointed at the door.

"You know who I am," I said, still angry.

She didn't answer.

"You recognized me right away. That's why you stared so long."

"I have no idea what you're talking about." She crossed her arms over her chest and refused to make eye contact with me.

"Really? You're not the teenage girl who sang *Cucurrucucu Paloma* on a panga in the Gulf of Mexico?"

Oh that got her. Her face crumbled and all her bravado evaporated.

It got me too because my anger dissipated. I took a step toward her.

My gaze slid to the door to find two men watching us. Her husband's neck was long and stiff like a peacock who had just been plucked. Rogan didn't reveal his reaction, but he never missed a detail. He'd cataloged every second in his memory.

"We need a minute alone," I said to them.

Her husband looked to her. Without lifting her eyes to him, she brushed him off with a wave of her hand. "It's fine, Thorne."

He nodded and closed the door, but I had to question a man who would so easily give in to a request like this.

Once the door closed, I took a deep breath and fought back the overwhelming urge within me to cut and run. I'd already hidden from this for years. Time to face the truth.

"Yo soy Primitivo de la Cruz," I said softly. *I am Primitivo*.

Her shoulders stiffened and her hands shook.

"Tu eres Magdalena Esperanza." *You are Magdalena*.

Her head moved slowly from side to side. "Ya te olvidé," she whispered. *I've already forgotten you*.

"No." There's no way she could've forgotten me nor I forgotten her. It was too big a moment in both our lives.

"Sí. Ya te olvidé," she repeated.

This girl had a serious case of denial going on. "I promised to find your mom and bring her to you. I never did that." Difficult words to say, but needed to be said.

She continued to shake her head.

"I looked everywhere. Searched all of Mexico. Covered the ground in Texas. Claudia's gone."

"Yesterday is gone." She turned her back to me and stared at a point far in the distance.

Was she even listening to me? I was making a huge effort to talk about shit I'd rather eat dog poop than talk about, and she kept denying it and speaking nonsense. "I avenged Claudia's death. Manuel and his men are dead."

"You shouldn't have bothered."

"They deserved to die for what they did to her."

"You wasted time and lives. She's not dead."

Aida Soltari lived in a fantasy world. The shooting didn't happen? Her mother never died? Whatever. Her insanity was her problem. Not mine. She needed to get a grip on reality. I just needed to say my piece and move on.

"Take my word I did all I could."

She spun and faced me again. "Your word is nothing."

I deserved that. I'd broken a promise, but at least she'd admitted to knowing me.

A long silence stretched out between us. Agony, frustration, and fear simmered in her eyes. She pushed it at me, expecting me to take it. Nope. Not my problem.

My eyes felt drawn to the closed door. The urge to bolt and never return grew undeniable in my chest. I hated this and everything about it. She was right. The past was gone. Today I had a job to do and bad guys to hunt down. What I did not have to do was convince a deluded diva that people had died.

An anguished cry came from her mouth, and she flopped forward. Her forehead landed on my chest. What the everlovin' fuck?

Her shoulders heaved with a big breath in. Her whole body shook as the air came out in short bursts.

Oh shit. Tears. My cue to leave.

Her hands gripped my biceps and squeezed. The feminine scent of her hair hit my nose. My hands came up instinctively, knowing she expected me to comfort her. She'd lost her mother, and it was my fault. But I couldn't touch her. The second I did, this became mine. The grief fell on me and I accepted it. Never. Grief was a wasted emotion. She said the past wasn't real? Emotions weren't real either. This was all a huge show put on by a world-class actress.

"I have to go, Aida. You give this to your husband. You talk it over with him."

She nodded into my chest.

"Goodbye." I stepped back and she raised her head, shocked eyes staring at me. What? Nobody had pushed her tears away before?

Welcome to reality, Aida. I don't want your shit. Find someone else to cry on. It's just snot on my shirt.

Chapter 6

RACING OUT OF THAT room like a bat outta hell, I didn't stop to look at her husband chatting with Rogan in the living room of the suite. What did they know? Nothing. Nothing about Primitivo and Magdalena. If the husband didn't spill, Rogan wouldn't even know about the bomb at her concert in Switzerland.

I stopped at the door and turned back to glare at her husband. "You don't have a security detail on her?"

The French guy stood and faced me. He straightened his jacket. Who wears a goddamn jacket in the Caribbean? "I'm her security detail."

I laughed. "You? A fart could blow you down. Where's your weapon?"

His face twisted in all kinds of confusion. What the hell did she see in this guy? "I don't carry a weapon."

"Exactly. She has no security. She needs a team implementing counter surveillance, decoys, and alternate routes. She needs twenty-four seven halls and walls, ballistic doors, panic buttons... Have you done due diligence on all her PAs, stylists, girlfriends, the staff of all the venues? Does anyone do social media analysis for her?" Shit. She needed a lot of work.

Rogan kept quiet, but his rapid eye movement showed him parsing the pieces together. She was at risk, and this guy was shady as hell.

French guy extended his peacock neck again. "She would never allow that. It's frowned upon in the opera world. One does not flaunt their status or show up with bodyguards. It shows a lack of trust."

What a sack of bullshit this guy spewed. As bad as her. Two totally clueless, superficial artsy types. Too worried about impressions to take basic safety precautions.

"From what I can see, she's been nominated for a Latina Choice Award. She's crossed out of the opera world into celebrity pop-culture. A place loaded with predators and criminals out to get her."

"This is true." He chewed his thumbnail like a child.

"She's also denying a bomb went off in Switzerland." I threw this out like a dart.

Rogan's jaw grew tight. Yeah, French guy didn't share the details, did he? What the fuck was this guy's deal? He allows her to talk behind closed doors with a man like me, and he doesn't tell Rogan key information about a terrorist attack?

"She says there was no massacre on the dock yesterday. She's unstable. And you let her call the shots? Stand up and be a man and take care of your woman."

He finally showed the proper reaction by pulling his shoulders back and getting a backbone. "I take care of her fine. What is your name anyway?"

Well, shit. We hadn't even met, and I'd nailed him as the perpetrator right away. "Falcon."

"I am Thorne. I take good care of Aida. The bombing and this tragedy all developed recently. But I hear you. She does need increased security."

The wrinkles in his forehead made him appear appropriately concerned.

"Good." At least we agreed on something.

"What do you suggest?" he asked.

Oh shit. I hadn't thought of that. Rogan could hook her up with some of his connections.

"We'll do it." Rogan stood to join the conversation.

"No, we won't," I answered back. We were about to cut and run and leave this mess behind. Let some overpriced celebrity security firm take her on. Rogan didn't do international work anyway, and an opera star most likely had to travel.

"Not a team out there tighter than ours. We'll keep her safe," Rogan said.

Shit. He'd picked up she meant something to me. But he spoke the truth. No one better than Z Security to protect her.

"I like it." Her husband smiled at Rogan. "Draw up a proposal and we'll negotiate a contract."

"Falcon, you head up the task force." Rogan turned to me.

"Fuck no." Goddamn. He'd already committed.

"No way in hell." Aida's voice sounded from the bedroom door. She stomped over to her husband and got right up in his face. "I don't want him on any task force. I don't want a security detail."

With her hips and ass in full motion, she was bigger than him. He was tall and lean and she was wide and curvy. A total mismatch.

"Honey..."

God, he turned into an even bigger wimp in front of her.

"No. The theatre is a refuge. We don't bring threats in with us."

"This is about keeping the threats out of the theatre. They blasted their way in last week. We need to take action." Thorne gave her a weak response.

"It was a freak accident. It won't happen again."

"And the shooting on the dock yesterday isn't related?" Thorne finally challenged her. Good.

"No." She threw up her hands in frustration. "It's got nothing to do with me. Terrorism is everywhere. I just happened to be in the wrong place at the wrong time. You are all overreacting."

I had to laugh at that. The queen of drama calling the kettle black.

"It's done." Thorne crossed his arms over his chest. "Rogan and Falcon will provide security for you. We'll make it work behind the scenes. Most people won't even notice." Thorne gave her a forced smile.

"We'll be invisible," Rogan said. His specialty. But I knew he wouldn't be traveling with us. Rogan would keep his ass in Boston to be with Tessa and his family.

Thanks for tossing me into the gator pit, brother. Invisible was not my forte. My specialty included intimidation with size, force, and a powerful rifle aimed at your forehead.

Whether we did this incognito or not, Magdalena Esperanza, or Aida Soltari, just became my problem again. For the second time in my life, I was responsible for someone completely out of my comfort range.

Chapter 7

AIDA (Magdalena)

"Week-two status update." Falcon's burly voice hit my ears as he flanked my right side. We'd arrived at the Metropolitan Opera House in New York one hour early, so he could do his obsessive checking of the place before the dress rehearsal tonight.

"Are you speaking to me?" Falcon hadn't said anything directly to me since the one-week status update where he scolded me and repeated his asinine list of schoolmaster-like rules.

"Security detail is ninety percent in place. Blaze and Diesel have a team on halls and walls. I'm on excursions."

"Lucky me." My dress rehearsal for the Met's production of the opera Aida counted as an excursion? The vocabulary Falcon used baffled me, as I was sure mine did him. I avoided asking him about it because I would not be the one to initiate a conversation that might bring up the subject of the last twenty-two years. If he served in the military, good for him. Inconsequential to today and the performance I needed to focus on.

"We vetted your inner circle. Thorne, Leticia, and Babette check out clean." He kept talking to me like a commander directing his troops.

"Of course." He had interrogated my husband, makeup artist, and the head of wardrobe for the Met like criminals.

"You frigid?" he blurted out.

"What?"

"Two weeks, one call to your husband. No titty pics, no phone sex. Frigid."

Ugh. What an ass! "That's none of your business. Continue with your report."

He narrowed his eyes, like he was trying to figure me out, then shook his head and moved on. "The cast is sixty-four percent vetted. There's eight hundred fucking people involved in this production." He spoke to the air like he was complaining to an imaginary Army buddy by his side.

"Well, yes, my dear. The Metropolitan Opera does everything on a mega scale. The opera of Aida has the largest cast of any of the operas they perform. Plus the orchestra, stagehands, and directors. It's an epic wonder." I swept my hair to the side as we approached my dressing room.

"We posted some false appearances for you on your website."

I stopped short and peered up at him. "You did what?"

"To throw off a tail." He kept scanning the area instead of giving me his full attention.

"I understand, but I have fans who follow me. What if they show up at those fake shows? I see no need to create confusion."

He looked down at me for the first time since we'd exited the vehicle he used to transport me to the venue. His gaze traveled over my breasts and stopped at my fists on my hips. "Do not question me or my methods. Follow along and don't say shit about it."

How rude? Falcon was consistently ill-mannered and uncouth. Thank goodness we'd reached my dressing room, and he'd be forced to wait outside.

Matteo, my co-star in the show, walked toward us, arms open wide. "Aida, my love. Are you prepared to die for me again tonight?"

Falcon moved his massive body in the way to block his hug.

Matteo stepped back and glared up at Falcon, who stood a foot taller than him. "Excuse me? Who is this?"

"Matteo, this is Falcon." I had to step out from behind Falcon to reach Matteo. "He's providing security for me."

His eyebrows rose as he inspected Falcon from head to toe. He was underdressed for the Met in his perennial black cargo pants and tee. He'd combed his hair back and tied it. His goatee appeared trimmed, but he still looked like a pirate you'd see on the high seas. "Yes, I heard about the bomb and the horrible incident in the Caribbean. I'm so sorry for you," Matteo said.

"Thank you so much." I turned to face Falcon. "I've known Matteo since Juilliard. He's my Radames. Don't stand between us." My fists were back on my hips and Falcon glanced at them. The corner of his mouth twitched up. What was it about my hips? "Did you hear me?"

His eyes moved back to Matteo, who spun my shoulders so I faced him.

Matteo embraced me with gusto. He ran his hands down my sides and patted my bum as he kissed each of my cheeks. "Aida, Aida. How I have missed my Aida."

We played Aida together six months ago, but the separation took its toll on me. Tonight was a homecoming and reunion of friends. "And I have pined through the long hot summer, eager to return to my Radames."

"Go now. Become Aida and I will be Radames and we shall die together and rise again." He added more kisses to my cheeks before flouncing away to his dressing room. Having him here helped calm my nerves. Opera fans picked sides, and I liked having Matteo on my team.

Falcon's cold stare at Matteo's back smothered the warm embers of Matteo's hug and reminded me of my house arrest.

"These are my friends. Many people will hug me. I have a reputation to maintain. Do not interfere."

He smirked. "Yes, ma'am."

His totally sarcastic tone told me he would stand between me and anyone else until after he'd checked their toilet to make sure it was clean.

As I sighed, Falcon opened the door and stuck his head in the dressing room. Over his shoulder, I could see the tips of Leticia's fingers waving hello to him. "Heya, Falcon man."

I pushed past him and shoved the door closed. His hand on the doorknob resisted until he'd finished checking the room. I brushed past Leticia and slammed the inner door to the bathroom.

What had he been looking at? My reflection told me nothing. I was wearing a blouse in copper silk. It had three wavy tiers at the wrists. When I put my hands on my hips, my fingers disappeared into the fabric. The flared sleeves swung back and forth like church bells. Add the peplum ruffle at the waist and I looked like the... Liberty Bell.

How infuriating? The man was exasperating and maddening.

I changed into my dressing gown, and my face frowned back at me in the mirror as I plopped down in the makeup chair. I had applied only eyeliner and mascara this morning. Leticia swiped a makeup remover sheet gently over my eye.

"Your bodyguard is hot." She dried my face with a soft cloth and took stock of my skin tone and puffy eyes. "You getting enough sleep?"

No. Sleep eluded me lately. "I'm fine."

"He's got that dark and dangerous thing nailed down. His body is fah-ine. Maybe a little big up top, but I wouldn't kick him out of bed. His ass is tight like a trampoline and those eyes. Mmm-mmm. I'd drop my panties just to get those eyes on me." She was a sweet African American woman with natural curls and gorgeous dark skin. Her makeup skills were unparalleled, and I requested her whenever I was in New York.

"He's driving me insane," I said to her.

She paused and her head wobbled the opposite direction of her neck. "Who cares what he does? He's fine. If my bae gave me a hall pass, I'd for sure use it on your Falcon man straight away."

Couldn't argue with her. Primitivo grew up to be even more attractive than he was at eighteen. He smoldered back then, but now, with his added height, long hair, a sexy goatee, and much bigger body, he flamed like a blowtorch.

"He's a draconian prison guard. He won't let me go anywhere alone. He ignores my preferences. I can't even go shopping."

It felt good to share my frustration with another woman.

"What's that?" She scrunched her nose and put her cute little face right up in mine like she planned to kiss me. "That breath coming out of your nose?"

"I'm sorry?"

"You still alive? No bombs going off this week? He is my new favorite person for keeping you safe."

Aww, Leticia was so nice.

She worked quietly for a while. She artfully applied a dark foundation, thick eyeliner, mocha lips, and the controversial bronzer that transformed me into an Ethiopian princess. Some theatre goers objected to the heavy bronzer to hint at black skin. They called me a weak imitation of the great Leontyne Pryce whose naturally dark skin cemented her as the original Aida. I'd been highly criticized for the makeup, but when we toned it down, the negative reaction was even greater. They wanted Aida to appear as a bronzed princess, and I was making a name for myself as the new Aida.

"Is he married?" Leticia dragged me out of my pre-performance thoughts.

Was he? He didn't wear a ring, but he could be married. Why did I feel a twinge of jealousy about an unknown woman who had potentially snagged his heart? "I'm not sure. If he were married, the travel and full-time nature of his job has to be stressful on a relationship." Either way I wasn't going to be the one to ask him. Unless forced to communicate, we maintained a tense silence between us. He did his job with cold calculated precision. I refused to acknowledge anything about him. Neither one of us went anywhere near the turmoil and my weak moment on St. Amalie. He texted Thorne to make travel plans and only talked to me for safety briefings.

The door opened and Falcon let Babette, the head of wardrobe, pass through. She waggled her eyebrows at me and held back a smile. When the door closed, she rushed over to us and whispered. "Your bodyguard is to die for."

"Oh please, Babette. Not you too."

"He was all business, asking me questions, his eyes seeing into my soul."

"Yes, well. He cleared you as safe to speak to me."

"Good. How are you feeling, Aida? How was your summer?"

She must not have heard about St. Amalie. "It was long and hot, but I'm happy to be back home."

"Good. You almost done, Leticia?"

Leticia finished powdering my cleavage and stepped back. "Yes. Now I'm done. Tah-dah."

"Thank you. The makeup looks sublime. You really are supremely talented."

Her face lit up as she packed up her case. "Thank you so much, Mrs. Soltari. I appreciate you noticing me and requesting me."

That's what we all wanted, wasn't it? To be noticed. To be requested. To be heard and acknowledged.

I stepped over to the dressing area and removed my robe. This left me in flesh-toned seamless bra and thong. Babette helped me into the corset that cinched my waist and pushed up my boobs. It was as painful as a straitjacket and not ideal for singing, but it looked insanely flattering on the stage. I'd learned to adjust my breathing to accommodate the corset. It always felt good to peel it off at the end of a show and massage the indents of the boning out of my skin.

The costume included not one but three pairs of tights. Now I had a big booty and large breasts, but this ensemble tucked and pulled everything into an extreme hourglass. Some reviews called me the pin-up Aida. They praised me for being a real woman and representing a time when women's bodies were rotund. Opera was one of the few realms where a full figure was desired and praised. Take that, haters. Old boyfriends and critics who said I would never make it as a performer commercially because of my body type. In the opera, my body fit Aida and many other roles in a way a skinny girl could never manage.

Babette slipped the dress up my arms and fastened the hidden velcro in the back. She took care to avoid smudging the makeup Leticia had so artfully applied to my breasts.

"You look incredible." She clasped her hands together. "You are going to blow this one out of the water."

"Thank you."

Chapter 8

———

WHEN I EXITED THE DRESSING room, Falcon's eyes traveled up and down, stopping at my cleavage, then up and down again. His mouth dropped open, but he didn't say anything.

"What's wrong, Falcon? Never seen an Ethiopian princess before?" I swiveled my hips left and right so he could see the entire costume.

"Threw me off for a second, that's all."

Yeah, right. I rocked his boat.

"You look good," he reluctantly admitted.

With a smirk, I walked away from him, and he followed me to the barrier of the backstage area. The production assistant stationed there looked up at Falcon and instantly started sweating. Three of this guy would not equal the weight of one Falcon. If he knew what I did about Falcon, or at least Primitivo before he became Falcon, he'd be even more terrified.

"Performers only beyond this point," he timidly mumbled to me while keeping his gaze to Falcon's.

Wonderful. A moment without my dark shadow. "Bye, bye, Falcon. See you after the show."

He grabbed my upper arm. "No."

His one-word sentences drove me nuts. Could he add a verb or a pronoun?

"House rules," I said. "I'll be fine. Only actors and dancers back here."

"You stay with me."

"Uh, well, I can't actually stay with you because you see, I am Aida, so the show will not start without me and you cannot pass this point, so I'll see you in a few hours. Why don't you go watch from the audience? You might find you enjoy it."

"If I don't go, you don't go."

He was so infuriating. This caveman shit was completely un-necessary and inappropriate for my world.

I wrenched my arm out of his hold. "Call Gaspar, please," I asked the PA. "Tell him I am being restrained against my will."

Falcon rolled his eyes as the PA made a call.

"Gaspar?" Falcon asked me another one-word question.

"Gaspar Evaristo? Tell me you've heard of him. He's only the most celebrated opera star that ever lived." I'd met him when I competed and won his opera competition for talented new artists. We'd bonded over our love of opera and when he heard I had no family apart from Soledad, he quickly fell into the role of surrogate father. He had no daughters with his wife, only three sons, so I filled a void in his life too.

"I may have heard of him," Falcon said quietly.

"Mr. Evaristo is on his way." Rivulets of stress streamed down the PA's forehead.

"And he's my father," I said to Falcon.

His brow furrowed. "Gaspar Evaristo is not your father."

"How would you know?"

His eyes grew angry and he popped a knee to shift his weight to one leg. "Are you kidding me?"

Ha! I liked getting a rise out of rude caveman Falcon. I decided to make this a game. From now on I'd do whatever I could to make his face look that contorted, confused, frustrated, and totally flabbergasted with me.

Gaspar arrived, looking concerned. "What is the matter, my child?" He was already dressed in his tuxedo and looked dapper with his silver hair combed back.

"This man is restraining me here." I pointed over my shoulder at Falcon.

"I'm her bodyguard. I stay with her wherever she goes."

Gaspar scratched his beard. "I see. But it's the rule of the house only cast members enter this part of the stage. I will watch over her."

Falcon's angry mask gentled. His eyes softened and his mouth turned up in a friendly grin. "It's an honor to meet you, Mr. Evaristo. My mother loved your singing. I respect your judgment, but Aida's been targeted by terrorists twice in the last month. My name is Master Sergeant Seth Hendrix, retired Special Forces sniper with the U.S. Army and a trained security specialist. I know what to look for, and I'm armed. I can protect her. It's my job. Now how would you feel, Gaspar, if she were hurt backstage because you weren't watching her and you missed someone approaching? What if you failed to defend her and she were injured or killed?"

This was the most I'd heard him speak. And never with respect to anyone in the time we've been together. He hadn't told me the name he'd adopted was Seth Hendrix. He'd only told me he went by Falcon. So much I didn't know about this man who'd been my silent companion and evil distraction for the last two weeks.

"I have an idea, mi corazon. Sergeant Hendrix can be a super," Gaspar said, trying to placate me.

"You can call me Falcon, Mr. Evaristo."

"And you can call me Gaspar." They exchanged a pleasant grin.

"No!" I screamed. "Do you see him? He's huge. He'll stand out like a sore thumb on the stage. He'll distract attention from me."

"Nothing can distract attention from you, my dear Aida, when you're on the stage. Being a super requires no prior acting experience."

"What are we talkin' about here?" Falcon asked, sounding a bit nervous.

"A super is like an extra," I said. "You would stand in the background and you'd be allowed to access the cast area, but I don't like the idea at all. I doubt we even have a costume that would fit you."

A costume that would fit him. Hmm.

"What kind of costume?" he asked.

"We could make you an Egyptian soldier," Gaspar replied. "That would be appropriate."

"All the supers wear tights." I delivered it like a punch. A man like him would never don tights and stand in front of a huge crowd. I won.

His mouth grew slack and he blinked as he stared at me. "Are you fucking kidding me?"

"Nope. Very tight tights. And a dance belt. A jock strap shaped like a thong." I grinned up at him.

He looked to the ceiling and shook his head. "Fuuck." When his head came back down, he looked like he was about to say no.

"Do I have to dance?" he asked Gaspar.

Oh, I didn't expect that answer.

"No," Gaspar replied. "You will stand in the back, perhaps some marching."

"I can march."

"I assume you can march better than any of the other actors on the stage." Gaspar gave Falcon a knowing smile. Falcon had disarmed him so quickly with his charm, yet he shared none of that congeniality with me.

A tense silence passed between us, and Falcon's Adam's apple juggled as he swallowed. "I'll do it," he said reluctantly.

"You will?" My voice squeaked up. No way.

He shrugged and a naughty smile grew on his lips. "You thought I wouldn't?"

"No." Total lie. His response to all this shocked the hell out of me.

His grin grew smug, like he could take on anything as long as he won a challenge against me. "I've dressed for many situations in various uniforms and costumes. I could not even explain them all to you, but a pair of tights is not the scariest of them."

Dammit. Damn it all to hell.

"Then we have our solution," Gaspar said with a smile. He must have seen my discomfort because he looked at me and laughed. He patted Falcon on the shoulder "Good to meet you, Falcon. Thank you for watching over her. She is precious to me and to the future of theatre. I'm glad you'll be close during the performance, and you'll keep her out of trouble during this perilous time."

Mama mia. Gaspar took Falcon's side? I should've guessed. My adopted father always worried about me.

"Is your makeup artist still free?" Gaspar asked me. "Check for someone in wardrobe to help. It's still early. Plenty of time."

"Fine." I marched back to my dressing room and surprised Leticia, who was still cleaning up her supplies and putting them in her makeup box.

"Gaspar wants Falcon to play a Egyptian warrior." I said it with the tone of a recalcitrant teen who had lost a fight with her father.

Her eyes blew wide as she glanced at Falcon. "He does?"

"Yes, as a super. Can you do his makeup and call Babette to help with wardrobe?"

"Ooh, girl. Is it my birthday?"

She scooted over to Babette's part of the dressing room and rummaged through some drawers to pull out a pair of men's tights and a dance belt, the athletic supporters male dancers wore to create the notorious idealized bulge in their tights. She held the items out for Falcon. "Put these on. Go back there. When you come out, I shall see my canvas."

He hesitated a second, and I challenged him with my eyes. I would love to see him squirm and back out right now. This had to be outrageously outside of his comfort zone. Falcon swiped the articles from Leticia's hand and strode to the bathroom.

She gave me an evil grin. "I love this job sometimes."

Falcon emerged a few minutes later wearing the tights and nothing else. The air sucked out of the room as Leticia and I feasted on the sight before us. Falcon was cut in every corner and plane of his body. His tattoos looked like war paint. Gaspar was right. He was the ideal warrior with phenomenal abs and pecs and muscles. His thighs alone were worthy of a solo performance. My core heated seeing him close to naked and what should feel vulnerable to him, but his demeanor had not changed. His legs were wide, his shoulders back. He looked nothing but sexy and confident. Oh my.

After feasting on his chest and legs, my gaze crashed and locked on his package. He was not hiding anything from us and—oh my lordy lordy good gordy—what we could see in his tights was X-rated. His cock extended from between his legs up to his left hip. Gods of Athena, help me. I could not stop staring. It had bumps. Small pointy bumps.

"Uh, ermm." Leticia was the first to form words. "What about the uh, dance belt?"

"It didn't fit," he said, deadpan.

Hmm. I could see why. His massive dick would poke out the top of a Lycra belt, and I was sure even the large wouldn't fit around his waist. The dance belt was also thong style. Falcon might be willing to don tights, and now I knew why, but he'd never put on a thong athletic supporter.

"Can I ask..."

He looked at me and his eyes burned through me. He had to see the heat in my neck, my pulse pounding, the absolute curiosity in my voice. "Ask what?"

"What the hell is in there?"

"My cock." He grinned.

Oh um. Well... "I mean, what are the points?"

He laughed. "The points are barbells. Piercings." He kept talking when I didn't respond. "Metal posts with balls on each end."

"Oh." I pulled my gaze from Falcon's fascinating package and focused on Leticia. Her lips pressed together and her eyes danced. She shook her head to break the trance and pulled up her phone. "Babette, we're gonna need a warriors' skirt with extra leather panels in the front." She ended the call. "Right. So. Lots of tattoos to cover. Have a seat."

In three steps, he was in the same chair I had sat in for my makeup. He spread his legs wide, and I saw his balls for the first time too. I didn't see any piercings there, but I sure wanted-ed to know.

I stepped back as Leticia moved closer. She was a brave girl. "This one we might be able to keep because it matches the theme." She pointed to two spears crossed at an angle. "What's this one?" She ran her fingers over crosshairs and a target with thorns at the points."

"When I made sharpshooter in the Rangers."

"Oh, the Army?"

"Yeah."

"And how long did you serve?"

"Twenty years."

Wow. Leticia had Falcon opening up and she'd barely met him. I'd spent two weeks with him and got nothing.

"You out now?" she asked.

"Retired three years ago."

"And now you do bodyguard work?"

He shook his head. "Private military contractor now."

"Like a mercenary?"

"Something like that."

So he and Rogan didn't only do bodyguard work. Was this a special assignment for me?

Leticia worked to cover the tattoos on his pecs with matching skin color. "Why do you have this bird?"

The bird covered most of his chest. The feathers of the wing tips crawled up his neck and ended below his ear. "Falcon. The fastest predator on earth."

"I see. Well, this one will take a while to cover. And we got these hairs here to deal with." She bent close to his chest. "Gonna spend some time on this." She smiled up at him and he returned it.

Was she flirting with him?

"This your wife?" She pointed to purple script that said *Eden*.

"Nah. Buddy's wife. Not mine."

He had his buddy's wife's name tattooed on his heart?

"You married?" he asked her.

She gave him a shy smile. "No."

I noticed she didn't mention her boyfriend.

"Did it hurt? Getting the piercings?" she asked him.

"Yes."

"Why'd you do it?"

"If you were married, I'd show you. But you're not, so it'll remain a mystery to you."

"Oh, you bad. You a bad, bad man."

He grinned. Holy Moses. Leticia drew all kinds of personal facts out of Falcon.

Why on earth would he prefer married women?

"Why married?" Leticia voiced my question.

"Safer."

Leticia washed her hands and stepped behind Falcon to brush his hair. He had gorgeous hair. Dark, shiny, and thick. It hung to the base of his neck.

"Safer than what? You're not afraid of angry husbands but you scared of single girls?"

"I'm not afraid of anything. Fear is a manufactured emotion. I control it."

Leticia pulled his hair back and wrapped it in a leather band. "You control your fears? Even when you served?"

"Especially when I served."

She finished with his hair and stepped in front of him again. "Where I'm from, we call that brave."

He shrugged. "Call it what you want."

They exchanged a look again. She was sweet and Falcon liked her. But this flirting needed to stop.

Thank God Babette knocked on the door and came in. Her eyes scanned Falcon in the chair, and she glanced down at the costume in her hands. "This might be too small, but it's the largest I could find. We might have to improvise a bit." She stopped short when she saw Falcon in his tights. "Oh my. He needs a dance belt."

"Didn't fit." Leticia and I answered in unison.

"Hmm. Stand up." She wrapped a skirt made of leather panels around his waist and fastened it in the back. "That works. Don't tell any other guards you're not wearing a belt."

Falcon nodded. I'm sure he wouldn't be discussing his undergarments with the other actors.

She fitted Falcon with a leather harness that traversed his pecs.

Babette added strapped leather sandals and a white cape that attached on each shoulder. She stepped back and admired her work. "Wow! You are one of the best-looking supers I've ever seen. I name you Hercules."

Oh dear lord, Babette had fallen under his spell too. "He's an Egyptian warrior not a Greek demigod." I found my voice to protest in some way to what was happening, but it made me appear petty and jealous, which I totally was.

"He still looks like Hercules to me." Babette handed him a round seven-foot stick with a fake spear at the end.

Falcon stood tall, puffed out his chest, and pulled his shoulders back. He set his chin in a regal pose and tapped his staff on the ground.

I swear to God I never would've guessed he had it in him but Falcon could act.

He reached for Babette's hand, bent at the waist, and pressed his lips to her knuckles. Babette and Leticia both sighed like schoolgirls.

As he did it, he raised his gaze to mine. Oh my lord in heaven. His eyes were molten and dark. They glimmered and my stomach flip-flopped. The heat from my neck spread through my chest and wetness grew between my legs. My body vibrated with his energy. He had seduced a room full of women with a few short sentences, a pair of tights, and his undeniable confidence.

How dare he? How dare he give me ice shoulder for two weeks, but in front of my staff, he pours on the charm? What the hell was his game?

Could he be trying to make me jealous?

Oh, that had to be it. Why else would he be putting on this show if it wasn't to get a rise out of me?

It totally worked too, but he'd never catch wind of it. Two could play at this game.

My body was revved and ready to perform. The spotlight would shine on me for the next few hours. Falcon would be forced to stand behind me and watch me. Matteo and I would light up the stage with our legendary chemistry. Even Falcon's untrained eye would notice it.

"Well, thank you, ladies. You've done a fantastic job again. I'd better get this super over to the staging area to get his direction."

"Bye, Falcon man. We'll see you before tomorrow's show, alright?" Leticia batted her lashes and waved goodbye to him.

"Until we meet again, my Hercules." Babette spoke with Shakespearean drama.

Falcon nodded, and began to stride out of the room. He stopped and paced back to the bathroom. He came out with his clothes under one arm and a gun in the other hand. He tucked the gun under the waistband of the skirt!

"You can't bring a gun on the stage!"

"No one will know. You won't tell will you, ladies?"

Babette and Leticia shook their heads in a stupid trance. Traitors.

And so Falcon and I walked out of the dressing room and strode through the Metropolitan Opera House in full costume.

The surprised PA allowed us to pass through the point he had stopped us before.

Lord help me.

Chapter 9

————

AFTER THE SHOW, HIGH from the rush of the performance, I soared on a cloud as we greeted the gold-star patrons in the foyer. A mixed crowd of older season-ticket holders and younger influencers from Broadway gushed over my iconic portrayal of Aida.

Falcon stood stone-faced behind my right shoulder, checking out each pen and camera as if it held a hidden IED. Earlier than I preferred, Falcon placed a firm, warm hand flat between my shoulder blades and gave a not-so-subtle signal, by the way of a push, that told me the time to socialize was over. I disregarded him and kept my feet planted as I leaned into the conversation with a co-star I'd be working with next month in Los Angeles.

Falcon bent down and grunted in my ear, adding a quick pat on my back. No words, but a clear message.

Enough. Time to go.

I excused myself and waved goodbye. He kept his hand in place on my back. A shudder trailed down my spine as the blunt pads of his fingers scrunched over my bare skin.

Inside the dressing room, I maneuvered out of his hold and spun to stare at him, seeking clues to his reaction to the show.

His eyes scrutinized me too. Intense blue beacons blinded me and amplified the adrenaline already coursing through me. His skin glistened with a fine sheen of sweat. The shoulder straps of his harness pulled tight against his rounded muscles. His legs spread wide and strong, not looking one ounce of feminine in his leather pleated skirt. The Egyptian warrior faced down the enemy—me—with no fear in his posture at all.

Oh my. What had I done? Using every tool in my arsenal to ramp up the sexuality of the performance created one of the best shows I've ever experienced. Amid the multi-tiered sets depicting sandy ancient walls and towering statues of gods and pharaohs, I poured on the emotion, lust, and desire in every scene. Matteo responded and played off me brilliantly. He touched my hips more intimately, pressed his groin to my backside more firmly, and turned the chaste kiss at the end into an R-rated extravaganza of tongues. Perhaps Matteo played along because he sensed my intention to drive Falcon mad. Or maybe he felt extra motivated tonight too. Either way, we rocked the dress rehearsal and impressed the small crowd in attendance. From the looks of him, Falcon was not immune.

A permagrin grew on my face. This was perfect revenge for his flirting with Leticia and Babette before the show.

He kept his eyes on me as he slowly removed his gun and placed it next to his spear on the dressing table.

The aquamarine of his eyes glinted in the fluorescent lights as he pinned me with a half-lidded gaze. "Quite the show, Aida."

"Well thank you." I bit my lip to hide how absolutely thrilled I was to get some kind of reaction out of the iron soldier.

He tilted his head and squinted as if trying to read my mind. "Do you love Matteo?"

Oh yeah. The jealousy gremlin revealed himself. Yipee.

"Not the way you're implying. My job is to convince the audience that I love him so much I would give my life for him. Apparently I have succeeded."

He blinked and moved his foot in a small, slow step toward me. "Do you love Thorne?"

The urge to answer his approach with a retreat overtook me, but the Aida costume helped me summon the bravery to stand my ground. The question about Thorne threw me off my game, but I couldn't let him get the upper hand here.

"What does that have to do with anything?"

"You didn't answer." He took another predatory step closer, his eyes flaring ice blue.

"Thorne has been my companion for years." This was not a lie, but also not the truth.

"Still didn't answer."

Uh oh. He had figured out my relationship with Thorne. Time to cover. "Of course I love Thorne."

"And he has no problem with you teasing Matteo and every man in that theatre till they went hard wanting to fuck you?"

I gasped. Surely, that did not happen. "Most of those men are gay." I shook my head.

"Doesn't matter. Anyone with a dick was sporting a chubby tonight."

Oh really? "Including you?"

"Most definitely me."

Oh.

Well.

He'd dropped his guard a bit by admitting I'd affected him. I made him hard. Good, because he made me wet and horny.

My gaze traveled down the rocks of his eight-pack and stopped on his leather skirt. My mind conjured up an image of the scene in there. A fully erect beast with barbells pressing against the fabric of his tights, his cock head trying to escape out of the top.

I cleared my throat and turned to the mirror to escape from the searching fervor in his eyes. "Then you should've worn the dance belt we gave you. It's meant to hide such things." Luckily my makeup concealed the blush blooming on my chest.

His reflection watched me remove the pins from my head piece as his massive body stepped close to my back, not touching, but close enough to make me tremble. "What game are you playing?" he asked me.

"I'm not playing any games." I lied. I was playing "Let's Confuse Falcon" and I planned to win.

"You sing," he said softly and inexplicably.

"You just saw me sing for hours, quite well I might add."

He nodded and leaned down so his gaze met mine in the mirror. "Do you moan?"

The air gushed from my lungs in a huge burst. "I'm sorry?"

"Does Thorne make you moan?" He somewhat repeated his question.

Oh no. This just crossed a line. He wasn't playing fair, using his eyes on me, his heat at my back, and bringing up the one thing I refused to discuss.

The past.

"None of your business."

His fingers grazed my hip and I flinched. He held them there for a second, likely waiting for me to push his hand away. I could have. He had touched me without permission or invitation, but evoking this reaction out of him made me feel powerful. I couldn't walk away now. We'd entered into battle. I froze, waiting for his next move.

He pressed his palm flat to my belly and snaked it slowly around and up under my left breast. Holy Mary Mother of God, help me.

My gaze was drawn to his giant hand spanning my ribs. For the first time in my life, I felt... petite. The pain in my chest forced me to suck in a huge breath. He had me forgetting to breathe.

He bent down and brushed my ear with his lips, his gaze moving from his hand on my body up to my eyes again. His eyes glowed a powerful blue against the sooty black edges of his eyelashes. "Are you gonna tell me the truth, or are we gonna keep playing our game where you lie and I pretend not to care?"

Was that the game he was playing? Was his ice sculpture imitation an act? It sure convinced me his heart was frozen solid. Falcon didn't care about anything except his job.

Which was me...

Oh.

I spun on him and had to lean back against the tabletop to get some space from the expanse of his naked chest. "Let me go, please."

He placed his hands on the table on either side of me, bringing his face parallel with mine. "Has anyone made you moan?" He smelled good, pungent like kerosene. "I got a feeling the answer is no. You're too busy keeping all your bullshit straight so you can manipulate men to doing what you want. You never let go and just moan. You're too up-tight."

"Uptight? Did you not see me on the stage. It was like one long moan."

"No. It was drama for effect. I'm talking about the real you. The Magdalena from Nuevo Laredo. Has any man ever had what it takes to get in there and make her moan?"

I turned my head to the side. Painful memories slashed through me.

Primitivo promising me he'd find my mom, telling me to sing, and telling me to moan.

If he doesn't make you moan, kick him out of your bed.

No. No one had made me moan. Not at all.

His eyes softened and his hand came up to my cheek, angling my jaw so I was forced to look at him. The corners of his mouth turned down and his face moved slowly closer. He kept moving closer, closer, till the warmth of his breath kissed my face.

I didn't expect the gentle press of his mouth to mine. Strong, full, soft lips kissed me. I didn't kiss him back or close my eyes. But as his lips started to move, my body took over. My eyes closed, my head tilted, and my hands came up to grip his forearms.

He kissed me with my cheeks cradled in his palms. I whimpered a weak protest. Never in a million years would I have guessed Falcon could kiss this sweet. And God I wanted it.

The sweet didn't last long because within a few seconds, his tongue forced my mouth open and swept mine into a wet, hot, penetrating kiss. The rough hairs of his goatee scratched my face. Overwhelming lust crashed through my system. Even with all the fabric between us, something huge pressed between my legs as he angled his hips closer.

Fire and ice. Cruel and kind. Distant and close. Forbidden and accepted. Totally physical but also completely ethereal. My hands caressed up his chest, fingertips exploring the heavenly dip and swale of each groove. Coarse hair on soft skin and billowing muscles.

His hand moved under my hair and gave a tug at the base of my neck. The demand in the way he yanked my hair crumbled what was left of my resolve to keep him at a distance. Regardless of the battle between us, I needed to kiss him more than I needed to breathe. And I had to give back as good as I got.

Each hungry swirl of his tongue drew me deeper into him like an aria that starts pianissimo and crescendos to an all-encompassing forte. We were flying with the music.

He moved closer yet, and my chest pressed to his abs. The leather of his skirt pressed the fabric of my dress into the skin on my legs.

His hand left my hair, and I felt massive palms at my hips lifting me up onto the makeup table like I weighed nothing.

I'd been with actors, singers, and dancers. Most of them equal in height to my five-foot-ten, and most of them smaller in stature than me. No one had ever lifted me by my ass like a babe from a stroller.

Putting me up on the table brought us closer to eye level, but he was still bending down to kiss me. My hands had full access to his back, and I scratched the bare skin, feeling it give under my fingernails.

His warm palm hit my breast and skimmed my nipple over the velvety green fabric of the dress. A promise of all the ways Falcon could touch me. Forbidden ways. Ways I shouldn't even be thinking of.

He pulled his tongue out and raised his head. He wiped his thumb across his lazy, plump bottom lip. His eyes had changed to a darker blue. His beard seemed darker and more pronounced. My God, turned on Falcon was a sight to behold. "Got a call from my boys on Thorne." His voice scratched, and he spoke quietly.

What? Oh shoot. Darn. Darn. Thorne. Where was Thorne this week?

"Said he spent the last few days in Orlando with a man."

Darn, darn, darn. That's right. He left to visit a new guy he'd been dating. He'd missed him too much to stay away any longer. Darn. He got caught.

"You followed Thorne?"

"Of course we did. He's the number one suspect for the murders."

"He's what? Oh my God. No. Thorne is not a murderer."

"No? What is he then? Cuz he's got a boyfriend down in Florida he seems to be heavily involved with, and he also plays the dutiful husband to you."

"Oh." Shit. I needed to get my game face on and lie to Falcon. Game face was hard when I felt like having an *O* face. *O* face would be one hundred times easier right now.

"You're a beard for him?" He asked his pointed question while I was thinking about my *O* face.

"I don't know what you're talking about." I knew what he meant, but I was avoiding the topic.

"A beard. You cover for him. Act like his wife so the public thinks he's straight."

"Of course not."

"Sure. Listen, you're hot as fuck and I'd really like to hear your moan because I'm sure it's beautiful with the kinda noise that comes outta your mouth, but I need you to admit the truth first."

Uh oh. He wouldn't make me moan if I didn't tell him my secret? This was highway bribery! Coercion! Racketeering! Someone arrest this man for being a thug. Well, I guess he was a thug considering who his father was and where he grew up. God, Falcon frustrated me to no end!

"I'm not interested in moaning for you, Mr. Hendrix, which by the way you didn't tell me was your name until I heard you tell Gaspar that."

"It's my name. Seth Falcon Hendrix. Don't forget it. Remind yourself in your sleep." He bent his head to whisper in my ear. "Seth... Falcon... Hendrix."

Gah! He was such an arrogant prick! Why did I even let him kiss me?

"In fact, now that I got my in, I want you to confess three things. Maybe four." He straightened and crossed his arms over his chest, making his tattoos come to life as his biceps bulged.

"You don't need to list them. You have no *in* and I won't admit anything to you. It can't be that good."

"Oh it can. And you want it."

I pushed his chest but he didn't budge.

"Admit you're a beard for Thorne."

I shook my head.

"Come clean about the six women who were murdered in St. Amalie."

Oh no. No. This wasn't happening. He wouldn't go there.

"Own who you are and where you came from."

Yes, he would go there. The man had no limits. Pain and anger warred in my stomach. I wanted to hit him and scream and yell, but I held it back. I put on my Aida warrior princess face and said firmly, "Never."

His mouth turned down into a frown. "Then we're done here."

He kept his eyes on me as he stepped away. He knew they were his greatest weapon, and he used them without mercy. His heat left me. My body, still on fire for him, began to cool with cold fury.

I was formulating a response when a knock sounded at the door. Matteo opened it and began to walk in with a smile on his face. He stopped when he saw Falcon blocking his way. Falcon's chest rose and fell with his deep breaths. His hands were away from his body, his shoulders hung low, and something huge made a bump in the front of his warrior costume.

My hands gripped the desk as if to hold me up. Or hold me back.

Matteo's gaze flitted from me to Falcon and back again. Boy, what a sight we must be. His shocked face morphed into a forced smile. He could not have missed the thick, heated, angry, sexy air in the room. "Aida, mi amor. May I speak privately with you?" Matteo's Italian accent and his deep baritone voice made everything he said intimate, friendly, and classy. The opposite of Falcon.

"Of course. Falcon, please give us a moment alone?"

Falcon's gaze assessed Matteo. He grabbed his gun and shoved it into the waistband of his costume. He gripped his staff and walked briskly past Matteo, warning in his eyes.

Matteo had smiled politely since he'd entered the room, but he dropped the act as soon as the door closed. "What the hell did I walk in on?"

With Falcon gone, I could breathe again, think again.

I stood up and straightened my dress. "Nothing. You walked in on nothing."

Matteo threw his head back and laughed. "Mi amor, I am no fool. The tension between you two blasted me in the face."

Oh shit. Darn.

"Matteo..."

"And here I thought tonight was for me."

"Let me..."

He held up his palm flat facing me and tucked his chin in a self-deprecating way. "No. I get it. You did this for him. I am the casualty on the stage next to you thinking I'd won the keys to the city."

Holy cannoli, I'd created such a mess.

I couldn't lie to him and deny it. I had used him to get to Falcon. And now I had to face the consequences.

"I'm sorry I misled you."

He raised one cautious eye to glare at me, but his lips twitched. He never held onto anger, and the performance drew a huge standing ovation. "What about Thorne?"

"Please keep this private. Nothing has happened. It's just a game we were playing."

"Oh this is so juicy. You're playing games with a super?"

"Not anymore. Just tonight. And he's not only a super. He's my bodyguard."

His stage makeup made his naughty smile and wide eyes look macabre. "Do tell. What kind of game are you playing with your bodyguard super?"

"I'm not. It has to stop."

"Who says? Let's drive him wild with jealousy at the next performance too."

That drew a chuckle from me despite the upheaval inside my head.

I wanted to say no. I should end this game with Falcon. The man exemplified the word *asshole*. We had zero chance of a future as a couple. If he continued to dig into my secrets, my fragile grip on my sanity would slip. I could lose myself, my career, Thorne's trust, and all the progress I had made toward finding my mother.

And yet, none of that mattered. I wanted to kiss him again regardless of the turmoil it would cause in my life. My inner muse wanted to see his piercings. She wanted to touch them and them to touch her. She ached to moan for him.

My inner muse confused me a lot. She had guided me to many correct decisions over the years. She'd helped me to pick songs and sing them in a way that captured the audience's emotions. But she'd also led me astray when it came to men. She'd picked losers for me and made me think I should love them when she was wrong. My heart had grown weary. She'd lost my trust from years of earning me broken hearts. She'd also romanticized Primitivo. She saw him as some kind of superhero who saved her and impressed her with his ways. Stupidly, she'd developed a crush on his memory.

But yesterday was gone. My inner muse was the old me. An illogical child motivated by insecurity and the need to be loved. Today was all that mattered. Today Aida was confident and secure. She could lock horns with someone strong like Falcon and win. Aida had declared war and victory would prevail.

"Tomorrow is going to be even hotter than tonight," I said with an evil smile.

"Yes, yes, it will. And pure torture for me because I adore you so."

"I adore you too, Matteo. I'm sorry you got dragged into this."

He waved a dismissive hand. "Don't worry about me." He came closer and caressed my upper arms. "Be careful, yes? Games like these can turn ugly fast. I know because I have done similar things, and my heart has still not recovered."

I smiled and pulled him in for a hug. "I will."

His hands caressed up and down my back, stopping at the base of my spine. "If he hurts you, come to me. I will ease your pain. Whatever you need. Sex, love, friendship, I am yours to be used."

Matteo's fans would die to hear him say such things. "Thank you, Matteo."

We had five performances over the next twelve days at the Met. Falcon would have to have superhuman self-control to hold out on me till then.

I'd break him.

He'd make me moan, and I'd give him no information.

It would be a dangerous battle royale.

But no matter what, I would not answer his questions, and in the end, I'd use him to get what I wanted.

To win.

Chapter 10

THREE WEEKS INTO MY bodyguard-imposed confine-ment, and Falcon hadn't allowed any excursions except the shows at the Met. I needed friends, air, food, and some hint at normalcy.

He'd said *no* the first two times I'd asked. I'd chosen the wrong times. I'd asked him after the show, *after* the kissing and refusing to answer his questions. He'd taken pleasure in denying my request and walking out with his hard-on under his skirt.

Last night, I'd changed tactics. I'd asked him after the show, but *before* he'd cornered me and tortured me with kisses. "Please," I said. "All I ask is dinner out with Soledad. She's my dearest friend, and I need to connect."

He'd agreed hastily, eager to advance to the kissing portion of our evening and replay our game; Make out until I nearly lose my mind, stop, ask the questions, refuse to answer, leave each other frustrated and angry, go home and masturbate.

So four nights in a row, we had done our battle and left the war room in a tense standstill.

Tonight was a dark night, and Falcon arranged a dinner at Giando on the Water with Soledad.

The last five minutes had passed awkwardly between Soledad and Falcon as they reunited for the first time in twenty-two years.

She had walked up to him and said, "Primitivo." Her face looked stiff and she didn't smile. Could have been her recent botox injection or, more likely, Falcon intimidated her with his scowl.

"Falcon," he answered back coldly.

"Right. Falcon." Soledad had waited a few seconds to see if he would say anything else. When he didn't, she had turned to me on the balcony and raised her pencil-thin eyebrows in an *okay, whatever* gesture.

We had hugged and ordered drinks, and now we were sitting together at a lovely table with a fabulous view of the Manhattan Bridge as we waited for our food.

"The critics are raving over your Aida run at the Met." Soledad sipped from her green-apple martini as we sat alone in the terrace dining area. We had the entire section to ourselves.

"Yes. Matteo is in prime form." I fingered the stem of my martini glass.

"So are you, my dear. The reviews all mention your seduction of the audience."

"Mmm." I glanced at Falcon standing guard at the door to the terrace.

"Looking at him reminds me of my glory days. I was young and starting out in a new country. My whole life ahead of me. Primitivo grew up to be an attractive man." She eyed him over her drink as she took a sip.

I loved Soledad. She was like my big sister, but a hidden tigress inside me bared her claws, then quickly retracted them. Yes, she had slept with Falcon twenty-two years ago, but she'd been married and faithful to her husband for nineteen years. She hadn't even spoken to Falcon since then.

"You can still have him. He prefers married women," I said.

Her eyes grew wide. "I would never cheat on Taye. You know that. He worships me and I him. I will never stray."

"I know. Taye is wonderful."

"I still can't fathom Primitivo working as your bodyguard. It's surreal. I don't know what I expected for him, but not this."

"For me too," I replied. Who would have ever thought Primitivo would reappear, not with my mother, but as my bodyguard?

"He can't be hurting for cash," she said.

"How would you know?"

"I can't say." She looked down into her drink.

"Spill, Soledad." Falcon had told me nothing in the three weeks since we'd reunited. He still chatted up Babette and Leticia before a show, but for me, nothing except for denying my excursion requests and challenging me to admit things I would never admit.

"It's nothing. It's just... He had money as far as I knew."

Falcon had money? "How much money?"

She leaned in to whisper, "It was rumored to be over twenty-five million all those years ago." She leaned back in her chair. "I have no idea how money like that appreciates."

Falcon a millionaire? The man who grunted and scratched his balls at least eight times a day? "I shouldn't think of him differently because you told me that, but I do." It made him even more attractive, and he was already damn hot.

"Why? What did you think of him before?"

"Well, I figured he did all he does for me out of obligation, but maybe not. He's doing a very thorough job. No one has come near me."

Her eyebrows dipped. "He's protecting you because he wants to?"

"I don't know. Thorne hired him. Falcon said no at first, but now he's crazy overboard about keeping me safe. He even wore a warrior skirt and tights to act as a super so he can be closer when I'm on stage."

She eyed him again and pressed her lips together in an ironic smile. "How noble of him."

The waiter brought me a steaming plate of shrimp scampi and placed Soledad's lobster and steak plate in front of her. I took a bite of shrimp and chewed on this new information.

I leaned in closer to Soledad so I could whisper. "Do you think he blew through twenty-five million, and he has to work as a bodyguard to pay his bills?"

Her nose tilted up and she inspected him from head to toe. "No. Look at him. He obviously doesn't shop."

I had to laugh because Falcon's black cargo pants and T-shirt made him appear underdressed for a posh Manhattan restaurant. Not sure why he didn't wear his suit tonight. He looked good in his uniform, but rocked a suit. "He was in the Army too, so he had a salary from that."

"Was he? Also noble." She carefully cut a bite of lobster, dipped it in butter and artfully placed it in her mouth.

"Now I'm curious what he did with all that money. Where did he get it? Certainly not from the Army. They don't pay that much, do they? He's so confusing. I don't understand anything about him."

Her pretty brown eyes stared at me for a long time. She must've had her eyes done. I didn't see one wrinkle. "I never told you this because it didn't matter, but now it's time."

"Time for what?"

"Time you know the truth."

My chest grew tight like a sponge after it's been squeezed dry. "You're scaring me. What truth?"

She leaned forward, elbows on the table. "He paid for everything. Our apartment in New York, your first car, our tuitions to Juilliard." She used a gentle tone, like saying it softly would make pulling the rug from under my feet less painful.

"He paid? Our tuitions? You said we won grants."

"I stretched the truth on that. Falcon gave us a grant."

I trusted Soledad and rarely caught her lying to me or anyone else. Everything I thought I knew about her changed when she admitted she lied. "Why?"

Soledad looked down, took a deep breath, and when she looked up into my eyes, I saw compassion there. "The money belonged to his father. He stole it when he left the country and asked me not to tell you. He wanted you to feel free from your ties to Guillermo. A clean break for both of us. Even after you became financially independent, he continued to send money, but I haven't touched it in years."

"When was the last time you used his money to help me?"

"Remember when you fell deep into debt when the Enrique scandal hit and no one would hire you?"

"Of course. That was an awful time."

"I used his money then to help you avoid bankruptcy."

A sheen of sweat broke out on my skin, and I had to force myself to keep my voice down. "Oh my God! Does he know about that?"

"No. I never told him anything about you until he called me a month ago."

Well at least there was that. Okay. I could handle this. Soledad did it to protect me. Falcon must've had his reasons too. Reasons I may never know. Maybe he felt guilty for not finding my mother. "So Falcon is my benefactor?"

"You could say that."

This changed a lot of things. Or did it? I felt humiliated and angry. And suddenly enraged when I realized...

"Wait a minute. So he paid for my schooling with drug money? Dirty, filthy money earned on the backs of the women who worked for Guillermo?" My own mother sold herself for him. Drug money, gun money, so many lives lost. I would've never accepted it if I had known.

"That's one way to look at it. I prefer to call it doing a good deed to give us a new start." She reached across the table to take my hand.

"I prefer to call it a huge lie." I pushed my food out of the way to make room for our hands on the table and placed my hand over hers. I didn't feel hungry anymore, and my evening out was ruined.

"What's going on with you two?" She glanced at him again.

"Nothing." He had been watching us, but when we looked at him, he turned his head away. He crossed his immense arms over his chest, and my gaze was drawn to his large, black watch. So substantial and manly on his corded forearms. I didn't see any concern or worry in his face. Hopefully, he didn't hear our conversation through some secret listening device.

"He keeps looking over here at you."

"He's supposed to do that. Part of his job."

"Oh please. Tell me everything. I told you the truth. Now you tell me." She patted our hands with her free hand, encouraging me to trust her.

"Okay. We've been kissing," I whispered the last word.

"Kissing?" Her head drew back and her chin tilted down. She looked at me like a schoolmaster looks over her bifocals—only she wasn't wearing glasses.

"Yes, four times. After the dress rehearsal and the first three showings of Aida at the Met."

"After?"

"In my dressing room."

"Really?"

"Yep."

"And Thorne?"

"Thorne doesn't know." Soledad knew my relationship with Thorne was open and I was free to kiss other men as long as the press didn't find out.

"Amazing." She released my hands and stared at Falcon in open wonder.

"Yeah."

"Just kissing?" Her brows came down and lines formed on her forehead. She had slipped into the role of caring mother and the wrinkles gave away her age.

"Yes. A little caressing," I admitted.

"He doesn't seem like the kind of man to stop at little caresses."

"Nope. It's more like groping to be honest. Then we fight and he leaves."

"He leaves?"

"He changes into his street clothes and drives me home in angry silence. Then he's off duty until the next show, and we do it again."

My vibrators ran out of batteries each night. I had to call down to the concierge to get more triple As sent up, but I was winning. He was close to breaking. I could tell by the grumble in his voice and the desperation when he attacked me.

"If I try to reach under his costume, he rebuffs me, moving my hands back up to his abs, which always distracts me and I forget what I was doing."

She laughed. "Well that sounds delicious."

"It's not funny. It's pure torture. Two more nights. Then it's over."

"Why?"

"I'm ending it."

"Why on earth would you do that? It sounds fabulous."

"He challenged me. It's a stupid game and it has to end."

"Tell me the details."

"I can't." How could I possibly tell her he wouldn't make me moan like he made her moan unless I admitted a lot of things I never wanted to admit?

"I love seeing you like this. It's like the old days. Remember Enrique and the games you played?"

"Remember the trouble I got into by playing those games? The public crucified me. Thus the almost-bankruptcy, which apparently Falcon saved me from."

She shook her head. "This is different. This is Primitivo de la Cruz! Guillermo's oldest son. The history between you two makes this epic. How absolutely fantastic!"

"It has to end." I had tonight and tomorrow to push him over the edge. He would break and make me moan without any answers to his stupid questions. "Thorne comes back after the final show. We'll be living as a married couple. I can't sneak away to kiss Falcon. I don't even want to kiss him anymore now that I know his father's money helped me become who I am."

"I would not end it just because Thorne returned. He will be happy for you too. And the money is in the past. Let it go. If it is over between you two, end it. But it looks far from over to me. You're just beginning."

"No. Not risking my heart like that. Not with Falcon. Far too dangerous."

"Danger can be fun. Why are you playing it so safe lately? That's unlike you. Seize the day and be your true self."

I moved my plate back in front of me to signal this conversation was over. I picked at the pasta but didn't take a bite.

Should I listen to her? Soledad always gave me good advice. But I also just found out she'd been lying to me for years. I didn't know where I stood with anyone.

"I'm not sure what is going to happen, but let's not talk about this anymore."

"Okay, but know this. I love you and I support you whatever choice you make."

"Thank you. I love you too. Very much."

Chapter 11

FUELED BY FRUSTRATION with Falcon, the next show went better than any of the previous ones.

The passion in my voice came from all the pent up hormones, the embarrassment about the secret money, and the consuming fear my detente with Falcon would end soon.

As usual, Matteo played off me with his unique brand of machismo and intoxicating voice, and we left the stage to another standing ovation and shouts of "Bravo."

With no words, Falcon attacked me as soon as we entered the privacy of my dressing room. Dressed as Egyptian princess and warrior, we banged around the room with our lips locked and hands clinging to each other in a fierce embrace.

I slowly snuck my hand inside my top and pulled my dress down, exposing my nipples to him for the first time. Second base. I had crossed the unspoken line in the sand.

It worked too because the second my nipple came out, his hot mouth locked on it and teased, swirled, and nipped. He mumbled in Spanish how it tasted like a fresh batch of tequila straight from the barrel. I'd never experienced the taste, but I assumed it was a delicacy in the breweries where he grew up.

I had him hooked. But, oh God, he had me on the line too because I'd say anything to keep his mouth on my nipple. Every brutal flick of his tongue shot sizzling arcs of lightning straight between my legs.

My nipples were a huge erogenous zone for me, and his rough treatment could bring me to orgasm without even touching me below. My arms quaked, my head fell back, but I didn't moan.

No, he wouldn't get that from me until I got what I wanted and he had nothing. Then I would be the winner and he the loser.

I reached under his warrior skirt, and my heart soared when he didn't push my hand away. I gripped his gigantic length through his tights. As I squeezed the frighteningly huge member, my teeth ground together to stifle a groan. The metallic balls stuck out like weapons, unforgiving and lethal. The tip reached to the waistband of his tights, begging to be freed.

As I reached inside and my fingers brushed the soft tip of skin pulled tight over the head, he snapped out of his nipple haze and his hand gripped the back of mine, pulling me away.

I growled like a caged lion as I did every time we reached this point. "Do not stop me." My words came out rough and angry, the threat clear in the sharp slice of my voice.

His head rose and he met my gaze with molten, fiery blue eyes, like a beast who had been lit on fire. "Admit your marriage is fake." He spoke to me for the first time since before my dinner with Soledad.

I'd fought hard to protect Thorne. He deserved my fidelity. But Falcon possessed unsurpassed skills of interrogation and an unbreakable will, probably ingrained in him by the military. I didn't stand a chance. I had to outsmart him.

Maybe I could give him this first one, and he'd give up on the other two. "Fine. My marriage is fake."

He grinned like he'd won. I guess in a way he had. "Progress." He kissed down my breast to take a nipple in his mouth again.

His lips trailed kisses up to my mouth, and his tongue dove in for his victory lap.

He ended the kiss and stared at me. "Why?"

I'd already chipped a hole in the bucket. Might as well let it flow now. "I had earned a bad reputation."

His eyes widened and a hint of anger flashed through them. He must not have read the old gossip about me.

"I'd been through several men. Famous men. They said I sucked blood like a vampire because of my teeth. A slut. None of it was true. I was the one getting my heart broken by men who disappointed me. In opera, there is a huge double standard. Men can do as they wish in their personal lives.

The sopranos and mezzos must be considered pure. The media portrayed me as unreliable because I couldn't maintain a relationship in my personal life. It's bullshit. I can sing consistently no matter what happens off stage, but they began a smear campaign against me as a lead. I went broke for lack of work."

His eyes changed as he listened. I'd shared very personal information with him. I trusted him with something he could use against me if he chose to. But I could see in his eyes, he didn't like the story or the opera world judging me negatively. Maybe it was his natural protectiveness, or maybe he didn't like me going through men, but a warm glow grew in my heart at his apparent concern for me.

"You didn't change your teeth?" he asked.

I'd thought about it briefly. "No. They make me who I am and any kind of procedure could affect my voice."

"So how did you end up married to Thorne?"

"Gaspar took pity on me. He is a compassionate person. He introduced me to Thorne and suggested we marry for appearances. Thorne's family is homophobic. They threatened to disown him if he came out. He doesn't care about them or the public opinion. Many dancers are openly gay, but he has a teenage brother who is questioning his own sexuality. Thorne wants to maintain a relationship with his parents until his brother is eighteen and can get away."

I took a deep breath. I'd never told the whole story to anyone before, and I felt drained having to verbalize the pain I'd endured the last two years as I fought to revive my career.

"Shall we resume?" I needed my mind off this and back on his pierced dick. I reached under his skirt again but he stopped me. Darn.

"Come clean about the murders."

I shook my head. I couldn't give him that. I just couldn't. I pulled my shoulders back and held my breath like I'd done every time he asked this question.

He eyes narrowed. "State your given name." His voice demanded I answer.

Why did he need this one? The one thing I absolutely refused to give him. "You say yours."

"Primitivo Borrego de la Cruz." He said it easily, like he didn't just admit to being the son of a murderous narco boss.

"You proclaim it so freely? You negate the existence of Seth Falcon Hendrix when you confess to being Primitivo."

His nostrils flared. "I don't admit it freely. Only to you. Only right now. It's who I am and all the negativity that comes with it. I am also Seth Falcon Hendrix and all the bullshit that comes with being him." He bent his head and stared at my naked breast.

I pulled up the fabric to cover my nipples. "What bullshit comes with him?"

He stepped back and when he looked up at me, his eyes had cooled. "Seth Hendrix is a sniper."

"You mean was? You're not enlisted now, are you?"

He shook his head slowly. "I'm a private contractor. Get hired to do sniper work. Not always for the military."

"You kill people? Are you evil like your father?"

A muscle in his neck pulsed and he took another step away. "Not like my father. Never like him. Don't compare me to him ever again."

"Okay. I'm sorry." I had been unfair. He'd shared something private with me, and I'd thrown his father's name in his face.

"Can I trust you to keep my given name confidential? My father finds out, he'll hunt me down and try to kill me."

"I won't say anything. We both have our secrets."

He nodded and looked around the room before his pretty blue eyes came back to me. "You have some hidden agenda to get revenge on me for failing to find Claudia?"

The pain of Tivo saying my mother's name rocked me to the core. My shoulders hunched and my arms wrapped around my middle. "You promised me you'd bring her back."

"Yeah."

"You didn't."

"No. I'm sorry." He sounded sincere and tired, like the apology weighed heavy on him.

"What happened?" I knew the answer would be painful, but I needed to know so I wouldn't keep wondering and blaming Falcon.

"I took my father's money. Left him with nothing. He joined forces with Manuel. I didn't have the skills to go in alone. Signed up for the Army. Perfected my shooting. Anytime I was on leave or not on a mission, I searched for Claudia. Couldn't find her. Assumed she was dead. Manuel and his men paid for her life with theirs."

This tore me up. Part of me wanted to thank him for killing Manuel. At least he got what he deserved. Another part hated Falcon for giving up the hunt for my mom, but also felt guilty that he sacrificed so much of his life to search for her. I'd relinquished my life to search for her too. We both tried. We both failed.

"She's not dead."

He stared at me with dark eyes, wrinkles forming at the edges. "I hope you're right."

He rubbed his face from forehead to chin. Grief came off him. Or maybe my grief had taken over the room. Either way, the raging hormones were gone.

"We're done here tonight." He stood and left me alone in my dressing room. Again. This time I was drained emotionally and physically. Fine. Let him leave.

We had one more night. One final showdown. I had only given in to one of his demands. He'd shared part of himself with me.

It was still a tie. I had not admitted my name even though we talked about the past. We didn't touch on the murders.

I'd recover from this and come back to win again. It's what I did. I always had strength for the final encore.

My inner muse wept. She didn't want this performance to end. She wanted to keep battling with Falcon through many shows.

No. Tomorrow this game ended. The Superbowl of battles. The fat lady would sing and the final curtain would fall.

HIS MOUTH HAD BEEN glued to my breasts for thirty minutes. My tights lay on the floor. Back in my dressing room after the last show of the run, my ass was on the table as he stood between my legs.

We had repeated our pre-combat preparations. The show had wowed the audience again. At the VIP greeting, Matteo helped me by staying close. He didn't go so far as to kiss me, but he'd kept his arm around my shoulder. Falcon's mouth had turned down each time Matteo whispered something in my ear.

Now, Falcon had my skirt pushed up, his hands caressing my thighs. He only needed to move his hand or his mouth to my core and I'd win. He'd make me moan without forcing me to give him what he wanted.

His head rose, eyes pleading, his mouth red and his jaw slack. "I want to eat your pussy for hours."

Good lord. "Yes, do it."

"You're gonna moan, mi carina. So loud we'll need privacy."

Yes! I won! "Okay. My hotel room. Let's go now." I caressed his head and gripped his ponytail at the base of his neck. My words were breathless.

"Come clean about the murders." His voice begged me.

Shoot. Darn.

"It's our last chance, Falcon. Let's not ruin it with that. Please just take me to my hotel. Don't ask questions."

"Answer the question and we're out of here. If you don't, I leave right now. I'm off this assignment. Done playing games with you. "

I chewed my lip as I stared at him. I'd pushed him too far. I didn't want him to leave. "Okay. I'll answer one more question, but that's it. I believe the murders were a warning sign to me."

He nodded, unsurprised. "What kind of warning sign?"

"I don't know. Maybe a crazy fan."

He gave me a dubious stare. Most of my fans were senior citizens or very tranquil people.

"Own your name." Good. He didn't ask more about the murders. He was as eager as I was to get through this part.

I closed my eyes. Fine. It wouldn't be a true loss if I gave in on this because I'd get what I wanted, which was Falcon to make me moan. I'd say anything right now to get him in bed.

"Alright. I will say it. But we'll never bring it up again."

"Works for me. Say it so I can finally fuck you."

I took a deep breath and held it, forcing each word out slowly. "I am Magdalena Claudia Esperanza." My voice broke off and I looked down at his hands on my thighs. "My mom was a whore. I lost her one night when a man tried to shoot up the brothel. I left Mexico without her. I loved her so much." Tears burned behind my eyes, but I fought them back with anger that showed in my voice. "Magdalena does not exist anymore." My fists clenched and opened. I couldn't look into his eyes. They knew too many details. "I'm saying it to you now because I want you to fuck me long and hard. I want to moan. I've wanted it since I was fifteen. Tonight is the night. Make me moan, Primitivo. Make me moan like no one has."

I looked up at him, and his eyes had softened. The heat was still there but kindness shined through. It reminded me of the way he'd looked at me when I'd cried all those years ago. He caressed my leg up and down gently and reached up to swipe a tear from my cheek. "Okay, mi paloma." I gasped as a word I hadn't heard in a long time brushed my ear. *My dove.* "Okay." He stepped back and handed me my robe. "Change quickly. We'll go to your hotel."

I sat in stunned silence as I watched the muscles of his back move. He took his gun and his street clothes with him into the bathroom. He'd remembered the song about the dove I used to sing. I had forgotten. But he'd remembered.

As I changed, I looked in the mirror. Fifteen-year-old Magdalena stared back at me, her hair loose, her lips red and puffy, eyes wet and shocked.

She clutched her robe to her chest, shocked by all that had just happened.

"Did we win?" I asked my inner teenager.

"Who knows? But I'm so freakin' excited. It feels like we won. It doesn't matter. Go get dressed. Go, go, go! Let me at him! And relax a little. Enjoy it. Whatever you do, don't get in my way!"

Chapter 12

FALCON

Never worked this hard for a fuck in my life. Never let a chick drag me along by the balls like this.

Aida engaged the grab-twist-pull technique, sucking me in with her curves, kissing me like she wanted me to own her, then pulling the vulnerable card at the end and shutting me down.

My masochistic side embraced the pain like jumping into a scalding hot shower.

Burn me again, baby.

Turn my balls cobalt blue.

I'll take it and come back for more.

Disappointed she caved tonight. I thought we'd carry on necking like teenagers indefinitely. When I'd found her waiting for me with her tights off, I knew the end was near.

Her defenses cracked when I'd attacked her tight pink nipples like a man possessed. Worked them hard, took my time, drove her to the precipice, and tested her again.

I wasn't surprised the nipple torture broke her resolve.

What I didn't expect was the rawness of the truth or the pain admitting her name would cause her. Genuine tears pooled in her eyes, not the ones she manufactured for her audience.

I wasn't prepared to see Magdalena confess she'd wanted me since she was fifteen. And I wasn't prepared for my reaction. Wanting to take emotion from her. I took emotion from no one. Always on them. Not my show, not my monkey.

But who could push away a captivating, strong-willed woman like Aida when she had her legs spread, her breasts naked, and her secrets on the table?

Even my frozen soul thawed a little.

Sure, guilt played a part of it. I'd failed to deliver on my promise. Not sure fucking her made amends for any of that, but it was all I could give.

I came out of the bathroom, and she had changed into a tight black skirt that ended in a ruffle below her knees. Oversized red flowers were plastered all over her black blouse. She looked luscious in the skirt and red strappy heels, but the whole ensemble was coming off as soon as possible.

Her skin glowed from washing her stage makeup off, and her eyes were wide and bright with the new makeup she had applied.

She stumbled as I grabbed her hand. I tugged her through the theatre to the SUV in the parking garage, strapped her in the front seat, and hit the road.

The emotion she'd experienced remained heady between us in the car, but as I channeled my thoughts to the various ways I wanted to fuck her, the air changed to pure sex. Definitely start with her on her back. I'd only had her sitting up so far. I wanted her on her back spread eagle before me. Let her feel the full effect of my apa and ladder the first time. She'd moan then. No doubt she'd moan the first time.

Second time on her hands and knees. More moaning. Brought a crop with me in case she was open to it. Not sure she'd get off on a stinging ass. She seemed a little self-conscious about her ample backside. She'd let me tease her tits though. She had taken the tapping, pinching, and biting like a champ. Not many women liked the stuff that turned me on, but she loved it. She didn't beg for more because she was holding back, but if she let loose, she'd be a wild animal begging for the crop.

And I was hard again.

She wiggled in her seat and fiddled with her hair. Her exotic scent filled the car. Smooth like rain forest and sweet like champagne. As the street lights passed over her face, all I could think was damn, the girl grew up hot as fuck.

I called up Blaze. "I'm on halls and walls for the canary tonight."

She gave me the one-eyed raised brow she did when I used the code name we'd given her.

"You sure? I got Oz scheduled to arrive in fifteen." Blaze always had trouble adjusting to last minute changes.

"Release him for tonight. I got it covered."

I heard steps and a door closing to block out the background noise. "She's married, Falc."

Blaze needed to keep his nosey ass out of this. "I know and it's bullshit."

"Don't fuck the mark. Rule number one."

I laughed because he lied. "Whose rules? Rogan's? He knows my M.O." Rogan didn't expect me to follow any rules except don't get caught.

"You want the surveillance cut?" Blaze asked, finally accepting this was none of his damn business.

"You wanna watch?"

"Fuck no."

Didn't think so.

We made it up to her room. I opened the door to let her pass. She hadn't said a word the entire trip.

She set her purse down on a small table near the door and looked at me for direction, that sexy vulnerable look in her big brown eyes. She wanted me to guide her through this? No problem.

"Bed."

She nodded and her ass swayed in the tight skirt as she walked to the back of the suite. She turned and stood in front of the bed, holding her hands clasped in front of her and giving me more lost lamb looks.

"Nervous?" I asked her as I stored my weapon near the exit.

"No."

She said no but my diva lied so much, she could barely tell reality from acting. Her gaze darted around the room and stopped to look out the windows. The New York skyline reflected in the glass. Intimidating. Not the stage where she was comfortable and knew her lines. Alone in a hotel suite with a dangerous man like me, she had to be second guessing.

"You changing your mind now we're here? No theatre. No costumes. This is the real you and the real me. We got all night and lots of privacy. Not answering any phones or doors."

She smoothed down her hair. "Not changing my mind."

Huh. Still seemed nervous. Insecure. "What's bothering you?" Not sure why I asked. I could take her, and she'd forget her nerves about thirty seconds after my mouth hit her lips. Plus, her psycho thoughts were not my problem.

"I'm fine. Ya know. It's just. You... you're really big... and hot. And you're who you are, and I'm who I am."

"We spent the last month establishing who we are. Something else going on here?" God, why did I even care? She'd begged me, she was standing in front of a bed, what was the holdup?

"My costume has a corset."

What the fuck was she talking about?

"I know. Almost made you wear it here, but didn't want to hassle with taking it off you."

"Oh, well, I mean. I could've worn it here."

What in the hell? Where was my confident diva? "What I want is you to tell me why we're talking about what you could've worn when it doesn't matter dick all as you're spending the night naked."

She looked down at her hand pressed flat to her stomach. "Um. Yeah, see..."

Fuck me. She felt self-conscious without a corset? This was about her body?

I took three quick steps and flung an arm behind her back. Her breath gushed out, and her boobs smashed against me as I wrenched her up. "You were pretty back then. You grew up to be stunning."

Her eyelids flitted, and she pursed her lips like she wouldn't take it.

"Weeks I spent wanting you. Watching you bewitch Matteo and the entire fucking cast, crew, and audience. Shit, my security staff won't stop going on about how hot you are."

"You don't have to do this." Her voice was timid and weak, not taking me at my word. This made me angry, and I didn't want to fight with her. I wanted to fuck her. Was she angling for an angry fuck and trying to piss me off? If she was twisted like that, she'd regret it in the form of a red ass for days.

"Have to do this? Do I look like the kinda man who does anything he doesn't have to do?"

"No."

Right. She got me. "And you know what all those men are entranced with? Not the size of your waist, which is my ideal size, by the way. I got no interest in a waist I can touch my fingers on both sides when I wrap my hands around it." I placed my palms on her hips, fingers back, thumbs on the slope of her ribs. It felt good too, her waist narrowing just the right amount. "It's your confidence. You may be acting or this is just a momentary slip, but I gotta be honest with you. This woman showing me insecurity about her body is much less attractive than the Aida who seduced me and had me hard for weeks. So can I get her back?"

A smile grew on her lips and her eyes closed half-way. "Yes," she breathed out. "Sorry. It was just temporary. Thank you for telling me how you see me."

I hitched one of her legs over my hip and walked her back onto the bed. "Don't get me wrong. Still think you're a hot mess and a batshit crazy diva, but it's fuckin' sexy how you own it."

Lying her on her back, I positioned her hips near the edge of the bed, exactly where I wanted her. I kissed her hard and within seconds, she was back to where we left off in her dressing room. Her legs squeezing my hips, our tongues battling, her hands skimming down my back and grabbing my ass.

"Mmm," she hummed her approval and lifted my shirt.

I lost her touch for a second to take it off and toss it to the floor. My hand skimmed her flat tummy up to her tit, finding her nipple and giving it a swipe over the fabric of her ugly blouse.

"Oh God." She was already making more noise than she had before.

"That's right, baby. Let me hear you. Let me hear everything. It's just you and me and the sky."

Unbuttoning her blouse exposed a black lace bra. Nice. I kissed her tantalizing cleavage as I reached around to get the hook undone. She helped me get it off and slip it down her arms with the blouse. Full, round, tits greeted me and dusky pink nipples, hard and ready to be teased.

I took one between my teeth and then the other. Her hips came off the bed. My dick twitched and pounded. Needed to get inside this woman fast. Time to end the weeks of taunting.

"I'll get back to these in one second." I sat up on my knees. Her hands flew to the button of my jeans. "Hands over your head. You watch."

Her eyes widened, but she slowly lifted her supple arms up.

I tugged her skirt down her hips. She had to wiggle, but her tits jiggled in a way I never wanted that skirt to come off. I'd forgotten her heels and had to bend to get those off her feet. I got them off and went back for her black lace panties. God, she looked fantastic naked. How she could doubt that was beyond me, but her body was sublime.

She lowered her arms.

"Keep your arms up."

She hesitated but I gave her a warning glance. She had to let me handle this. If she hadn't moaned before, she was probably ruining it by rushing and worrying about pleasing whatever loser she was fucking.

She slowly raised her arms and her tits angled up. "You are fucking gorgeous, woman." My cock jolted behind the buttons of my jeans, fully hard now and near ready to blow.

"Now spread your legs and relax."

As she opened her legs, she revealed a perfect pussy glistening beneath a thinly trimmed patch of hair. Sexiest thing I'd ever seen, her sweet wet cunt waiting for me. I wanted to dive in and fuck her with my tongue.

Her gaze landed on my crotch. She watched me unbutton my pants and whimpered.

"You been wanting to see my cock up close, haven't you?"

"A long time, Falcon. Since I first met you."

I opened my jeans and she gasped when she saw the metal jewelry for the first time. I had a one-inch open ring through the frenum, the apadravya pierced my urethra. Two half-inch titanium balls on that one. The Jacob's ladder had three lower gauge barbells down the underside with quarter-inch balls on either side.

I let her gawk for a second, but not long because fuck the waiting. We had a lot of ground to cover, and my diva needed to moan for me.

I tossed my jeans and climbed on top of her naked body. I kissed up her tummy to her mouth without touching her with my hands. She kept her arms up and legs wide as she kissed me back.

Hot as fuck kisses. The woman and I kissed for hours and I could still kiss her more. I don't know how long we went on like that but the whole time my dick was pulling me to her cunt like a divining rod to water. She panted into my mouth.

"You good and wet for me? Cuz I don't think I can wait another second."

"Yes. So ready." She squirmed as much as she could with her legs wide. So sexy.

Slowly I lowered my hips till the tip of my cock hit her mound. Still hovering over her, with one hand, I guided the cool balls of the apa to her clit.

She arched her back as I rubbed it over her sweet little nub.

"Oh my God. That feels amazing."

"Yeah, baby. Yeah. More?"

Her hands clutched the sheets as she growled.

As slow as I could manage, I slid the underside of my cock over her swollen clit. When her hot wetness hit my cock, I groaned. "So wet. Gonna dive deep into that shit."

"Yes," she breathed.

Skin slipped on skin and my shaft fell deeper into her folds as the rungs of the ladder flowed over her clit like speed bumps in a parking lot. Everything was slick and hot and excruciating because, my God, I needed the real thing.

Her hands came down and gripped my shoulders. Her thighs squeezed me tight, and fuck if I could stop her. My whole world revolved around the rutting going on between us. I bit her tit to stave off my orgasm and bring on hers.

When my cock was covered in her juices and I thought for sure I'd blow on her stomach, her mouth dropped open, but no sound came out. The muscles in her neck grew tight, she held her breath and God, she was beautiful on the edge of orgasm. My dick ached to pound into her but I waited. Her moan needed to come first.

"C'mon. Give it to me."

Pressing harder and faster on both clit and tit, it was like rubbing two sticks together to make fire. "Sing for me, Aida."

I raised my head and moved my face to her cheek so I could hear it all straight from her mouth directly in my ear.

Her chest heaved and she let out the breath she'd been holding. Her gloriously long moan started as a high keen and changed to a guttural grunt. Her hot cunt wrapped around me and milked me, begging me to let go too. No, no, no. I had to grit my teeth to keep from blowing a load on her navel. Damn. This was for her, not me. She needed a man who gave without taking at the same time. She needed me to care about her orgasm and help her enjoy it to the fullest.

I lightened up the pressure but kept teasing her until the ripples stopped passing through her.

She moaned again as her body went limp. She'd been holding back on me before, but now she let it out and it was loud and gorgeous.

Totally worth the wait. Worth everything to hear Aida moan like that.

Time for a condom because I needed to get my dick in there. "Hold on."

She mumbled something and tossed her head side to side. Took all my concentration to get the condom on without ripping it, but I managed. Never been so hard in my life.

Oh shit. The crop. Could she handle more? One way to find out. I grabbed the short, stiff leather crop from my pack and climbed back on her.

Lifting one leg, I rested her ass on my knees. I slid the tip in and groaned. So good. So tight and wet.

Her closed eyes opened and startled. "Oh my."

"Feel good, baby?"

"God yes. Amazing. Keep going."

"Brought a crop to tease your tits. You open to that?"

"How did you know tonight?"

"Had a feeling it would be tonight. Also had a feeling you'd like the crop on your tits. You let me know if it gets to be too much."

"Yes." Her head fell back to the bed, and she raised her arms again.

With just the tip and the apa teasing her entrance, I started slow and gentle with the crop on the underside of her tit. She didn't flinch or draw back.

"More. I like it. More. Of both."

"Okay, baby. Okay."

I picked up the speed of the crop, tapped her harder, faster, and closer to the nipple as I worked my tip all the way in. The pressure popped as the apa breached the entrance.

"You good?"

"So good." She panted. Her hands came down and gripped the sheets. She looked down at the crop working her tits and threw her head back with a moan.

Her sweet pussy sucked me in, and her hips tilted, begging me to go in deeper. I moved the crop to her nipples and kept up a steady rhythm. Took all the control I could muster not to ram into her. That would hurt us both. I would love it but didn't want her to feel pain the first time.

And good God! Three more pops of pressure and I was balls deep in Aida.

"I'm in."

I kept the crop at her nipples, one thumb to her clit and started to move slowly. Her cunt engulfed me like a tight velvet glove. The barbells wiggled, adding to the overall pleasure.

I started to pump then. I needed to thrust. I'd waited too long. I wanted it to last forever, but I knew I couldn't. We had all night. We were definitely doing this again soon.

I picked up the speed and my spine tingled. She groaned like she was close again.

"Come on my cock, babe. Come on my cock."

She moaned loudly, like a song, prettier than any I'd ever heard. Her pussy clenched around me over and over for what felt like an eternity. Her juices gushed everywhere and smacked with our thrusts.

I stopped the crop as her orgasm faded. I rose over her and kissed her. My hips moved of their own will. Pumping, thrusting, ramming. Each stroke massaging my cock with her slick, hot walls. Fucking heaven inside Aida.

Her final moan came into my mouth, and I swallowed it. It fed the prickling at my balls and demanded to be released. It rushed up through me, and I moaned into her mouth. My hips jerked and it all spilled out of me. Rope after rope poured out into the condom as my cock twitched and emptied deep inside of her.

In that moment we were just two people sharing bliss. No names. Only man and woman sharing in ecstasy as God intended. Our bodies were made for this. Her body was made for mine.

More endless strokes to drag it out, and I collapsed on top of her.

She laughed and wrapped her arms around my back. Her legs squeezed me in a tight hug. I thrust in and out a few more times to let her feel the slow effect of the piercings. She trembled and trailed her nails down my back.

"Thought I'd die if I didn't come inside you."

"I think I did die a few times there."

I laughed and held her under me. "You moan as beautiful as you sing."

"Mmm. Thank you."

"Be right back." I got up, disposed of the condom, and prepared a warm washcloth to clean her up.

She didn't move as I wiped her.

She rolled to her side, closed her eyes, and pulled the sheet up over her tits. Her lips curled up at the edges in a content grin.

Usually, I'd leave. No contact after sex. Less chance of them getting attached.

But I was on duty so I might as well sleep in the bed with her. No point in getting dressed to go stand in the hallway. She'd be safe with me next to her.

So I climbed in behind her and tucked her sweet ass up against my groin. She wiggled and my cock started to fill. But she needed rest after her performances. Both of them.

I wrapped an arm under her luscious boobs, and she snuggled her back into my chest with a sigh. Her hand moved from where it was holding the sheet, down to rest on my wrist. Holding on.

She smelled like hair and sweat and sex.

The crop had fallen to the floor in our fucking.

Magdalena Esperanza.

Knew she'd be beautiful.

Didn't know she'd be so damn tempting.

Chapter 13

THE TUG OF THE PIERCINGS left a lingering pain that was nothing short of exquisite.

Now, sitting in a chair by the window, watching the black of night morph into slate gray over the skyline, I downed the whiskey I'd found in her mini-fridge.

After sex, when I should have been enjoying the release of pent-up sexual tension, the black abyss in my soul took center stage and killed any fleeting pleasure I'd found.

The absence of something tortured my conscience. The unsatisfied hunger I couldn't name wouldn't let me sleep.

Lavish hotel rooms and opera houses were not my scene. Wealth like this led to greed and poison.

I needed to leave. Blaze and Diesel could handle her. No one had attempted any attacks since we'd provided a presence. A deterrent was sufficient to protect her. It didn't have to be me.

This bodyguard gig delayed my plans to return to Mexico. Killing Manuel and his soldiers had decimated my father's numbers, but I'd slacked off. I needed to take names and make a list of who would die next.

"You look bummed out for a guy who just got laid."

I turned to see her watching me. Couldn't make out the details of her face, but the sheet highlighted the alluring curve of her hip.

"Go back to sleep."

"Tell me what you were thinking."

"I was thinking I like you when you're sleeping cuz your mouth isn't asking me questions."

"C'mon. Spill. It had to be intense from the look on your face."

"Was thinking how you live up here. High above the real world. Looking down on the slums and gutters where I hang out."

"You think I'm a snob?"

"No. Just a different life. It's good. I'm glad. I'm happy you have all this." She came from nothing and earned her wealth with her talent. She deserved it.

"I'm happy too."

Why did I care that she was happy? Was I any less guilty if she was? Why did I want to stick around and figure out the answers to these questions?

"What's your understanding with Thorne?" I asked her.

"My understanding?"

"He has a lover in Florida. You seem okay with that."

"Yes," she answered tentatively.

"But you said tonight was our last chance before he comes back to town."

"He usually stays with me in my suite. We sleep in separate beds. I won't have the privacy I have now."

"Thorne comes back. You pretend to be his wife. Who fucks you?"

"I have an eclectic collection of vibrators when I wish to please myself."

That was so fucked. "And he's celibate too? During the times you live together?"

"Yes. I believe so. We keep each other company. He's a good friend."

"Still. The arrangement sucks for both of you."

"It's a little lonely at times."

"I need to leave."

She remained quiet. The sound of the heater clicking on filled the room. The water ran in the toilet.

"Well, good. Adios, Primitivo." Her fake diva voice sounded forced, a hint of pain in her tone. The first time she'd spoken in Spanish to me. Couldn't blame her. The sun hadn't risen since we'd fucked, and I was making my escape.

"I got shit to do."

She turned her back on me and pulled the sheet up over her shoulders. "Then go do whatever you have to do. I'm not stopping you."

I downed the last of the whiskey and looked around for my stuff. Needed to pack up and get the hell out of here.

"You live in the past, Falcon."

She spoke the truth. I lived in the past. Fighting a decades old war. A war I couldn't win because even if I killed my father, someone else would rise up. Just like Afghanistan. Just like Syria. Same shit. Different day.

I left my glass on the table and stomped around the room in search of my clothes.

As I slipped on my pants, her voice hit my ears. "I could make arrangements with Thorne."

I froze and looked at her, my pants half buttoned. "What kind of arrangements?"

She turned around and looked at me. The sun had risen enough that I could see her face. "He would have another suite in the hotel. He would allow me to take a lover if I wanted."

Was she offering herself to me? "And do you want to?"

"Yes," she answered matter of factly.

Oh yeah. She was putting herself on the auction block. "You want more of my titanium cock?"

She laughed. "Yes."

I finished with my pants and sat down in the chair again. She wanted more. I never fucked available girls more than once. But she was technically married.

"You're basically available," I said.

"That's true in a way. I can't marry someone else unless I divorce him, which neither one of us plans to do."

"You could fall for me."

"But I won't."

"How do you know?"

"Clearly we aren't meant to be a couple. I live up here with my fake husband. You live down there, playing Don Quixote with your father."

Huh. Don Quixote. She knew me better than I knew myself.

"I'm starting rehearsals for my first Broadway musical. I do not have time to start a relationship with my hot bodyguard or explain to the press that said bodyguard has a titanium dick and I'm banging him behind my husband's back."

She sounded sincere. Twice before I'd attempted a no-strings sex arrangement and twice the girls could not keep their emotions in check. That was all before Eden.

"Rogan's first wife got attached."

She sat up in the bed, her eyes wide with shock that I was sharing stuff about my closest friend.

"Not in a good way. In the worst way. Even though he married her and loved her, she still couldn't let him go." I hadn't talked about it in years. Images of her funeral still haunted my dreams. "She died. She couldn't let go and she died. So you see why you can't get attached?"

"Because I'll die?"

I had to laugh through the grief. "You have zero control over your emotions. Your life is a stage."

"I resent that. I assure you I am in total control of all my actions."

"Right."

"Give me the access to the piercings. I'll enjoy them without attaching emotion to it. Acting only on the real stage. Not in my bedroom. Or your bedroom. Or wherever we end up."

She manipulated people. She'd find a way to get around it. "Don't put any of your baggage about your mom or your career on me."

Her head reared back. "I have made a concerted effort to avoid discussing my baggage. You have relentlessly teased me and forced me to talk about it. Stop interrogating me if you don't want to hear the answers."

Ha. I liked her spirit. Strong. Sexy. She was offering herself to me. More sex. No relationship. No emotion. "You make arrangements, I'll fuck you on your hands and knees. Tie you up. Take the crop to your ass. Listen to you moan all day, all night."

Her eyes filled with heat. "Um, well... I'd like that too. Are there any um... limitations with those things in your cock?"

"Limitations?"

"Can you take a blowjob?"

"Hell yes."

She nodded and smiled triumphantly. Like she'd won. "I'll make arrangements with Thorne."

"Deal." Wait. I needed an out. "Temporary. Until you're safe. After that, I return to charging windmills."

She giggled. "Okay. Now come back to bed. I'm cold. You're a nice blanket."

Those kinds of orders from her I could follow.

I stripped off my pants and climbed behind her, wrapping an arm under her breasts and tugging her up against my groin. "We're starting right now." Her breath hitched and her legs squeezed together.

Then I fucked her on her hands and knees. Made her ass red with the crop.

She moaned.

And I had a fucking arrangement with Aida Soltari.

I WORE HER OUT. SHE took it like a boss and passed out. Gave me a chance to check her room.

Colorful picture frames had been carefully placed on a shelf outside the bathroom. One picture showed her with Gaspar and Soledad outside a theatre hall. The snow fell around them as they huddled together in their wool coats. Aida wore her headpiece from her Aida costume and smiled as she embraced her friends. Gaspar's arm behind her back supported her waist. His other arm wrapped around Soledad's shoulders. They looked like a happy family. A fake family, but still enjoying their time together.

Two more framed pictures of her with Soledad. Another with her and Thorne. With the wind blowing her hair, his hands held her face as he kissed her forehead. She closed her eyes and accepted the kiss like a present. Sweet. Like a brother would kiss a sister's head. Not like a husband would kiss a wife he loved.

She had adopted friends and family who cared about her. She'd done what I told her. Sing, laugh, enjoy her second chance. She did it. She let the past go and made a life for herself like Soledad had done. Good for her.

I thumbed through her closet. She had the color cacophony she always wore slapped together in a messy rainbow. Aida celebrated color and wasn't afraid to own it.

My closet had a nice selection of weapons organized by caliber and ideal shooting distance. The clothes in my dresser had three colors, black, denim, and camo.

In the corner of the closet, tucked behind a rack of clothes, I found a gold box with turquoise and yellow paint. Looked like an antique from ancient Egypt. Inside she had stashed a plastic baggie. The paper towel inside it crinkled at my touch. Oh shit. Drugs? Was she being targeted by a dealer?

Inside the bag, little plastic wrappers. Lavender and magenta balls. Godiva chocolate truffles. Well shit. Aida hid her sweet tooth. From who? Thorne wouldn't like her eating chocolates? She needed to put that crap out in some expensive bowl and let it sit right on her coffee table. If she liked chocolates, she should eat them.

Either way, glad they weren't drugs.

In her underwear drawer, I found her vibrators. Holy fuck. She owned a rainbow of vibes. Bunny ears, pocket rocket, wands, and dicks of all colors. She wouldn't be needing these during our arrangement.

Everything else looked clean. This case was looking more and more like a fan stalking her, but we hadn't found anything unusual online. She hadn't received any threats. The attacks were too organized to be pulled off by one person.

I made my way back to the bedroom and watched the sun touch her cheek. Who the hell was blowing up her concerts and executing women at her hotels?

I sat next to her on the bed and stared at my feet.

Not sure what led me to look there. Maybe instinct or the experience of having sat on evidence many times throughout the years.

I curled down and scanned under the bed.

Bingo.

A laptop case.

I'd wait till her dinner date with Thorne tonight then send Diesel and Blaze to retrieve it.

Chapter 14

AIDA

Thank God for Thorne. The man was a saint. He flew into New York two nights ago, and we'd talked about making arrangements for Falcon and me to have a secret rendezvous without letting on to the public.

Thorne loved me. Thorne would do anything for me. Even marry me to save my reputation. So when I asked him if we could sleep in separate suites from now on, he jumped at it.

"Of course, darling. I'm so proud of you. He's big and scary, and you didn't let him intimidate you. Was the sex mind-blowing?"

"Absolutely mind-exploding."

"Fabulous." He leaned in to whisper even though we were alone in my hotel suite. "I heard he has body jewelry."

Talking out loud about what happened felt odd. Especially with Thorne, who had been my lone male companion for the past two years. "Where'd you hear that?"

He held his hand out in front of him and inspected it. Flakes of white skin hung from his cuticles. He had chewed the nails down to red nubs. When he saw me looking at them, he hid his hands in his lap. "Dancers talk. A man like him shows up in tights, everyone is going to take notice of what he's packing. Word is he didn't wear a dance belt, and piercings could be seen poking out the fabric."

My cheeks felt hot, and my legs squeezed together remembering the first time I saw Falcon in those tights. All the male dancers wore a dance belt to smooth out the details and create an unassuming, if not exaggerated, bulge. Falcon walked out and provided Leticia, Babette, and me with an unexpected lesson on male anatomy.

Thorne leveled his pretty green eyes on me. "I want this for you."

I shook my head and looked away. "It's not anything. Just sex."

"Whatever it is. I want it for you. I'm sure you're worried like hell you'll get your heart broken again, but we have to take risks. We can't hide behind each other all the time." He frowned and a deep sadness filled his eyes.

"Are we talking about me or you?" I asked him.

He pressed his lips together before he answered. "Both of us. We're both hiding."

"And when we hide, it doesn't stop the pain, does it?" I reached out and took his hand in mine, rough edges and all.

"No, sweetheart. It doesn't. The pain is still there cutting like a knife." He tried to pull his hands away, but I held tight.

"Any news from Alfonso?" I asked him.

He'd been seeing a new guy in Orlando who had ghosted on him.

"No."

We hugged and I whispered in his ear, "We'll get through this together. I love you."

"I love you too, Aida."

———————————

LAST NIGHT, THORNE stayed in a separate suite while Falcon and I spent the night exploring all the ways his titanium cock could please me. He encouraged me to climb on top of his tremendous body and ride him as I brought myself to orgasm with my hand. He tied my hands to the bed, and we played with the crop again. My soul finally felt free to be the sexual person I was meant to be. No worries about performance or if he was using me to get ahead in his career. We were just two people who really enjoyed each other's bodies. And he told me so in colorful ways.

Tonight I had to focus and prepare for the Latina Choice Awards.

I had won my first nomination for my pop ballad "Ya Te Olvidé." Nervous did not begin to describe the butterflies in my stomach.

Leticia came to the hotel to do my makeup. "Where's Falcon man?"

"He's spending his day attempting to turn the Jacoby Theatre into a fortress."

She laughed. "Good luck with that. I'm glad he's still watching out for you."

"He is."

"How shall we do your makeup tonight? Sultry and smokey or clean and fresh?"

"Let me show you my gown and you decide." I'd picked a daring couture Juan Ronaldo design for the evening. As I removed it from the dress bag, my stomach flipped. What the heck was I thinking picking a sheer black dress with strategic rainbow beading that only covered my private parts?

Juan had contacted me and convinced me the dress would get attention. I was hesitant at the fittings and kept asking him to add more of the gems. He'd agreed to an extent, but refused to let me cover up his design. It really was a work of art.

"Oh girl. That dress is going to make an impact! Definitely sultry and smokey. Sit down. Sit down."

I placed the gown on the bed and sat in a chair by a mirror when a knock sounded at the door. Thorne hobbled past Blaze, who was on duty guarding the hallway. "Darling, I am feeling quite green around the gills." His skin looked paler than normal as he clutched his stomach.

"Oh no. What's wrong?" I walked up to him and supported him by the elbow.

"I don't know. Food poisoning? Malaria? Whatever it is I can't go to the awards with you."

"I'll be so lonely without you."

"I'm so sorry. I will make it up to you. I have an ideal replacement."

"Who?"

"Falcon." He waggled his eyebrows at me.

Oh gosh. "No. Don't go there, Thorne."

"You said he's being paranoid about tonight. He can't get closer to you than by your side on the red carpet and at your table for the ceremony. Shoot, if you win, take him up on stage with you."

"No! Are you crazy?" That would feel too much like a date, and I was under orders not to get attached to Falcon. We had to keep it restricted to the bedroom. "I'll go alone. Not unusual for me."

"Too late. I've already talked to him and he agreed. He'll pick you up at five. And he'll be wearing a tuxedo." He bit his finger. "Can you imagine him in a tux?"

I could and I wanted to bite my finger too.

"Ooh, child. I'm sticking around to see that." Leticia put her makeup brush down and sat down on top of the desk, folding her arms like she was settling in for the wait.

I rolled my eyes at her and looked at Thorne. "Are you really sick?"

"Yes." He buckled over again and moaned.

"Thorne. Don't do this to me."

"You'll be fine with him. I'd better return to my death bed. Toodles." On his way out, he stopped and turned back. "Take pictures for me."

"No."

"Bye, bye, Leticia." He waved and closed the door quickly. God, I loved the man, but he could be so annoying.

━━━━━━━━━━

LETICIA INSISTED ON staying to help me put on the gown and finish my hair. She worked slowly too, chatting up a storm so she could catch a glimpse of Falcon in a tux.

When the knock at the door sounded, she popped up and scurried to open it. She held up one hand for me to stand right where I was, lined up, and slowly opened the door so she was behind it.

I meant to say something but the words stuck in my throat. Falcon looked sophisticated and sexy in his tuxedo. It fit him perfectly. The silk lapel and stripe down the leg accentuated his height and broad shoulders. He wore a thin black necktie over a pleated white shirt and silver cufflinks on stiff French cuffs. No cummerbund or vest, but he didn't need anything else. He'd smoothed his hair and tied it at his nape. His goatee was trimmed neatly and shorter than usual. He stood tall and strong, his face serious. His eyes rounded when he saw me, then narrowed and went over the details from head to toe. By the time he finished, they'd grown molten hot.

"Falcon," I said, not knowing what else to say.

"Leticia, you can leave now." Hunger broiled in his eyes.

She slowly came out of her hiding spot behind the door. "Okay, bye." She grabbed her stuff and walked to the door, keeping her eyes on Falcon's broad shoulders the whole time. She bit her finger like Thorne had done and scooted out.

As soon as the door closed, he said, "That dress is deadly."

I stood frozen with jitters and immobilized by Falcon's sudden presence before me.

"If we had time, I'd fuck you in it first, but we gotta go now. Next time, I'll plan better and give us at least an hour to mess up and redo your hair and makeup."

My ears heard him giving me a compliment, talking about sex. My brain merged his words with the upheaval in my belly and churned out panic. The dress made me look fat. Or slutty. He thought I thought this was a date. He expected me to win. If I didn't win, I wasn't a legit singer. I was just another opera star trying and failing to cross over to popular music.

"It's not a date," I blurted out.

His brows drew together. "Didn't say it was."

"No. I mean I don't want you to think that I think it is."

He looked to the ceiling and mumbled something I couldn't hear.

"I don't expect to win."

He took a step toward me, but I held up a hand. I didn't want him near me. "I won't win tonight."

He stopped and stood staring at me like an alien speck of dust. "You think I give a shit if you win? Easier for me and the team if you don't. It's challenging enough to cover you when you do the song, but if you win, I'm dealing with another location change in the middle of chaos."

"Oh." I hadn't even thought of the logistics for him.

"I wasn't going to tell you this, but we received a threat today."

I gasped. "What kind of threat?"

"An email through your website." He stared at me with tight lips like he was done talking.

"And? What did it say?"

He looked around the room before he spoke. "Aida Soltari must die."

Oh my goodness. My hands shook and my heart raced in my chest. They really were out to get me. "Who sent it?"

"Came from an ISP in Russia. Diesel and Oz are working on it, but we don't have room for you to spin psycho crap about winning or losing. We have to be sharp and on point. If your thinking is twisted, I can't trust you to make good choices. I need you to cooperate. By cooperate, I mean be fucking confident. Plan your reaction if you don't win, but I think you will. I got a strategy set up with the team for that outcome. Be prepared to react quickly if something goes wrong, but please do not fuck this up with crazy-ass insecure negative thoughts. You look hot. Let's get the fuck out the door."

I opened my mouth, but didn't speak. What could I say? He was right. And smart. And I felt stupid, so I just said what he wanted to hear. "Okay."

He nodded, the anger still in his eyes, as he held out his hand for me to go ahead of him.

He shifted into silent bodyguard mode as we took the elevator down to the parking garage and he buckled me in the back seat. A car pulled up in front of us, another behind us, and we headed to the Jacoby theatre like the Queen and her Royal Protection Squad.

THE LATINA CHOICE PRODUCERS went overboard on the "Latinas in Love" theme of the show. Romantic hearts and twinkling lights hung from the ceiling. Arching hearts on the stage glowed in shades of pink to deep red. Tables set for two lined the audience, chairs situated so couples sat side by side. I still felt nervous about the threatening email, but I did my best to put it out of my mind and enjoy the evening. I trusted Falcon to protect me if something went wrong.

They played romantic Latin music through a luxury seven-course meal before the show. By the time the waiters cleared the dinner and turned on the stage lights, my nerves had settled. I enjoyed sharing my first meal with Falcon. He didn't talk at all, and his eyes constantly scanned the crowd. He barely ate, but I felt comfortable and safe with him by my side.

When Enrique took the stage, Falcon's eyes stopped scanning to settle on him.

"You dated him?" he asked.

"Yes." He must've seen the details of our ugly break up. Enrique and I burned hot, and he might have been the only man who came close to making me moan, but we fought as much as we fucked. Not long after a huge fight, I'd found he'd posted images of himself on vacation with another Latina beauty. Someone much more famous and much skinnier than me as they kissed in the blue waters off Peru.

"You break it off?"

"No, he cheated."

Anger flashed in his eyes.

"Stand up, everyone. Move your body!" Enrique called through the microphone as his song picked up, and the beat pounded through the floor. The house lights went down, and the theatre converted into a dance club.

I stood and pushed my chair back. Falcon looked twice when he saw I'd moved to the aisle to dance. With a clear intent, he took his place behind me. Keeping a safe distance, always on guard. By the time the chorus of the song hit, the house went nuts. Everyone cheered and sang the song Enrique had topped the charts with this year. Falcon stayed still, but my hips swayed to the music. You could not listen to this song and not dance. I put my arms up over my head and enjoyed the moment. Enrique knew exactly how to get a crowd fired up.

The heat and weight of Falcon's hand hit my hip. I gasped as a hot tingle vibrated to my soul. He was touching me in public for the first time. I took a small step back to bring us closer and that was all we needed to set the fire between us to flame. The soft fabric of my dress brushed against the roughness of his tuxedo pants. I might have even felt his hips move with mine. Oh God, dancing with Falcon in public was something I never expected to happen.

His low voice hit my ear. "He doesn't deserve to be the dirt on your shoe."

My heart thudded and my body swayed.

"If he's the one threatening you, he dies tonight."

My breath caught in my throat, and I turned to look up at him. His eyes stayed on the stage. "Um, no. It's not him. Please, uh, don't kill him."

He nodded and looked down at me. He gave me the shortest flash of a smile before his gaze focused behind me and turned angry again.

A cameraman and a production assistant moved in front of us. Darnit. Falcon stepped back and the spell was broken.

"You're up in twenty, Aida. Need you backstage now," the PA said as the song ended and the lights came up.

"Okay."

I HADN'T PERFORMED "Ya Te Olividé" since before Falcon and I began our arrangement.

The song had long been my anthem.

Every time I sang it, I declared my freedom and independence from the pain of my youth. I'd not only forced myself to forget Primitivo, but my family and the tragedy I'd left behind. Recently it had come to help me get the murders out of my mind, so I could perform without breaking into tears.

When the grief started to bombard me at the sound check, I fought it, putting up an imaginary fence between present and past. Found and lost. Life and death. Sex and love.

During the sound check, the fence worked. I didn't cry. I'd remained professional and I'd gotten through it. Tonight, with Falcon taking me on this non-date, sitting at a romantic table with me, and then putting a possessive hand on my hip to protect me from Enrique, the fence came crashing down like he'd driven a tractor through it.

He'd breached the boundary, and with it all the ugliness I'd been trying to forget slammed into my heart.

Manuel taking my mother.

A shooter in the brothel in Mexico.

Primitivo killing his brother.

The pain of twenty-two years of loss.

A bomb at my concert.

Six dead girls on a dock.

Ya Te Olvidé.

I've already forgotten you.

No. I had never forgotten. I'd only blocked it out. His reappearance forced me to face every dirty detail. Each time he touched me with his incredible hands or tantalizing cock, he reminded me.

Maybe he hadn't forgotten me either.

He'd sent money.

No. I couldn't entertain such ideas. I had to prove to him I could keep my end of our deal, but deep inside, I didn't want an arrangement. I wanted him to care. I wanted his soft eyes on me. I wanted to be free to fall in love with him like my inner teenager had done years ago.

And so the words stuck in my throat.

The band stalled a beat then played the lead in again. I needed strength to get through this. But where would I find it?

As they repeated the intro two more times, I imagined a cinder block wall around Falcon.

As he stood guard just off stage, the blocks stacked around him like a fortress. I added another wall of blocks in front of the first because Falcon was strong too.

When it reached the roof of the theatre and boxed him out with no windows or doors, I found my voice.

The first few notes sucked, but at least I'd begun.

By the time the chorus hit, I'd connected with the audience. The past evaporated. The future disappeared, and the current me sang to them, the people who had nominated me and this song. I owed it to them to keep it together for the next three minutes.

And I did. I sang the song with all my heart. I sang for today and Falcon stayed locked behind his block wall.

As soon as it ended, of course, he broke out. Because no wall could keep Falcon back. He'd break through any barrier put in front of him. He clapped and smiled at me with pride in his eyes.

I walked over to him with my head down. His arm came around my back. "You did good, mi paloma."

I didn't want that to mean the world to me, but it did.

"Go get your award."

"What?" Looking up, I saw his gaze aimed out at the stage. "You won. They called your name. Go get it."

Then I heard the crowd cheering and the replay of my song.

I ran out to the podium. A billion eyes stared at me, but my brain was fried. I felt like I was floating above the room watching this happen. I let my gut speak for me.

"Who would have thought a girl like me could make it this far? But here I am holding this award chosen by you. You chose me. Thank you from the bottom of my soul. I can't express my gratitude to my manager, the record company that took a chance on an opera star, and my family. Soledad, Thorne, and Gaspar. I love you with all my heart. You are my everything. And to the man who keeps me safe despite my efforts to thwart him. Thank you."

I walked back to Falcon, and his hand found my waist again for a moment before the PA ushered me away to the media room.

"I can't do any media," I said to him.

He nodded. "She's going to skip the interviews." Falcon spoke for me.

Thank God because I could barely form a sentence.

"Okay, Mrs. Soltari," the PA said. I'll tell the production co-ordinator you were sick and had to skip the interviews."

"Thank you."

THE MOTORCADE FELL in line in front and behind us and we drove home in silence. When we reached my hotel, Falcon came in and closed the door.

He moved toward me, but I held up a hand. "Stop."

He didn't. After three long strides, he wrapped an arm behind my back and mashed us together. "What's wrong?"

"I'm just drained. The song, the award, all the emotion and excitement on top of the threat. I'm done. I can't take any more. I can't take you right now."

His eyes scanned mine from left to right and back again, looking for an answer.

"I need to process a lot of very deep emotions tonight. I'm soaring and crash landing. There's going to be ugly tears. You don't want to be here for that."

He didn't let me go. His eyes weighed the pluses and minuses of staying. If he stayed, he'd have to listen to me, but he might get laid. If he left, he wouldn't have to listen to me, but he certainly would not get laid. "Alright."

He released me and I felt the loss of his warmth. I knew what he would choose. He'd never willfully share emotion with me.

"I'll be in the hall."

I nodded, but I wouldn't call him. I needed to keep that cinder block wall up around him.

I set the award on the table and took off my dress. As soon as I hit the shower, the tears flowed. Mostly for the victims in St. Amalie and their families. I felt the grief for all of them. Then I cried for my mother and all the women forced into prostitution. I felt the weight of it all on me.

All the other memories took their turn in my brain. I couldn't stop them with an imaginary wall. If something wants through, it finds a way.

After I cried it all out, I heaved a final sigh and fell into sleep.

SOMEWHERE IN MY DREAM, I heard a click. Soft foot-steps, the rustling of clothes, the bed dipping, and a giant body sliding up behind me. It was a nice dream. In my dream, Falcon wrapped an arm over my hip and worked his big warm hand under my breast. His breath in my ear soothed me. We were one. Everyone was safe. No one was dead. Twenty-two years hadn't passed.

When I woke, the bed was empty.

Chapter 15

"WE NEED SOME PRIVACY, if that's alright?" I played it off like I was still upset about the awards show. I wasn't, but I needed some space from Falcon for other reasons.

Falcon glanced at the numbers on Thorne's closed hotel suite door. "Okay, but I'll be right out here."

"Thank you."

If the woman Thorne had rescued and brought here was my mother, all this subterfuge would be worth it.

Falcon opened the door and let me in. He scanned the living area and closed the door again. I ran to the bedroom where Thorne sat with a woman. She wore the clothes I had given Thorne to bring to her. A black hoodie, a clean white T-shirt, and sweatpants. Her curly dark hair billowed out from her head, covering her face as she cried into her hands.

My mother had straight hair. This girl looked in her twenties, much too young to be my mother. But no matter, she needed help and maybe she could lead me to my mom eventually.

I approached her slowly. Thorne looked up at me from where he kneeled in front of her. He questioned me with his eyes. Is she your mother?

I shook my head no.

He nodded. We'd been through this many times. We didn't expect to find her, but we had found this girl and could help her.

I kneeled down next to him. I didn't touch her or force her to look at me.

"What is your name?"

"Isabella." She mumbled into her hands, but she said the *I* like an *E* with a Latina accent.

"What a beautiful name," I answered in Spanish. "I know you're scared, but we are here to help you. You are safe. You can calm down. We won't harm you."

She stilled and peeked up at me through her hair. Makeup smeared down her cheeks. I placed one hand softly on her shoulder. She cried harder. I hugged her, fighting back my own tears. This was so fucked up. How could someone treat another human being like this? Forcing them to have sex, controlling them, selling them like livestock. Breaking the trust of a family, the trust of humanity. Her basic rights had been stolen from her. Ivan's group of pimps were ruthless gaslighters. They used beatings, threats, drugs, anything they could to force the girls to perform. They obeyed out of sheer terror. But no one chooses this life.

The door burst open. Three men with guns entered the room like an avalanche. Thorne stood up. I grabbed Isabella tighter and wrapped my body around her to protect her. Her pimp had followed us here or even worse, Ivan's assassins had cornered me in a room and this poor girl would die with me.

"What the fuck?" An angry voice filled the silence after the crash. I didn't look, I just braced for the shot that would end my life and hopefully spare Isabella.

"Stay back," Thorne yelled.

A long confused silence passed. I held her tighter to me. Her curly hair crunched under my hold.

"Aida, look at me." A familiar voice.

I raised my head to see Blaze, Diesel, and Falcon standing above us. The raised ends of their rifles slowly lowered to the floor.

"Who is she?" Falcon asked me.

"She is my mother," I answered.

"She is not. Who is she?"

"She's a woman. Like me. Like my mother. She's been trafficked. She needs my help."

They relaxed their stances and looked at each other. While they adapted to what was happening, I released Isabella and spoke to her in a soothing, calm voice.

"You are safe. They won't hurt you. Please, listen to me. You have been trafficked, your dignity stolen, your choices taken from you. I'm here to tell you that is over. You can begin to heal now."

I peeked up to see Falcon's shocked face. All three of them stood motionless and listened to me talk to her.

"We are going to get you some help. We'll take care of food, clothes, a place to stay. You won't be arrested. Your pimp won't find you. You're not going back. You will heal. It will be difficult. The first few weeks are the hardest. But you'll have a team of mediators, teachers, social workers, and doctors at your side. And me. You will have me. I promise to stand by you and help you through this. I've helped lots of women and girls and you must trust in me that it will all be okay."

Falcon's whole face had softened. He finally saw what I was doing here. He got it.

The three guys sat down in chairs and continued to watch us. Slowly, she raised her head. Accepted my words, nodded, and said, "Thank you."

We exchanged more tears to shed the pain and hugs to start the healing.

With a knock at the door, all three commandos stood alert again.

"It's okay. It's the volunteers from the shelter. They'll get her settled in a room. They'll process her papers, get her some identification, try to find her family, and get her into therapy and rehabilitation. Let them in."

Falcon opened the door after checking the peephole.

I placed an arm behind Isabella's back. "These are mediators. They've been where you are and know how you feel. You can trust them."

The meditators came in and held their arms open to her. "Her name is Isabella," I said.

She stood and walked toward them.

"Sleep tonight, Isabella. Sleep safely. I will visit you tomorrow."

She left with the volunteers.

Falcon came to me and towered over me. His firm hand landed on my back between my shoulder blades. I looked up at him. "You come with me."

———————————

HE USHERED ME OUT OF the room and back to my hotel room. When the door closed, he planted his fists on his hips and nailed me with a vicious glare. "You lied."

"About what?"

"I asked you what you know about who is targeting you, and you said you thought it was a fan. You had no idea. Tell me the truth now or so help me God, I'll leave and you'll never see my cock or my face again."

His anger intimidated me, but I wouldn't let him see it. "Calm down. No need to use your dick as a weapon."

"Calm down? My team, a highly trained Special Forces tactical unit, has been racking their brains trying to figure out who's after you. Many agencies are working full-time on the murders in St. Amalie, and you have a connection you didn't share?"

Okay. When he phrased it like that. "Isabella is not a connection."

He took a step closer, towering over me like an irate father. "She's not? How many women like her have you rescued?"

I looked away. "Thousands."

"Thousands?" In all my previous efforts to shock Falcon, I'd failed, but this? This shocked the hell out of him.

His voice scratched, and his brows drew down. "And you send Thorne on thousands of missions like that? Unarmed?" He pointed to the door in the direction of Thorne's room.

I stepped back to get his wrath off my skin. "I usually go with him, but my bodyguard hampered my plans, so he went alone." I flicked my wrist like this was no big deal.

"You go with him?" Oh boy. If he wasn't mad before, he was now.

"Yes."

"Do you know how incredibly stupid that is? God, the pimps could be there and kidnap you, rape you, turn you into a victim in a second. You're playing with fire."

"The pimps usually aren't there. If they are, Thorne goes alone, makes the payment and waits for the pimp to leave before he makes the girl an offer. If the pimp doesn't leave, we give the woman the number to the center so she can call us when she's alone."

"So you leave your calling card behind? No wonder you're being targeted." He paced the room, his shoulders high. "You manipulate people. Thorne does this for you? What other dancers do you have out on the street doing a job the police should do? Trained professionals deal with this stuff. They know what to expect. They prepare. You two walk in there like lambs for the sacrifice. Completely unprepared and unarmed marching into the slaughter."

He was totally overreacting. It wasn't like that. "I've been doing this for ten years."

"And how many times in those years did you come close to dying?"

"A few."

"Right. And how did you get out of those?"

"We got lucky. Ran before we got caught. Thorne runs a distraction and I sneak the girl out."

"Thorne runs a distraction? Thorne? The fucking ballerina who can't even tell his parents he's gay?"

"Don't attack Thorne. He's a brave man, and we know what we're doing. We're helping people. We're making a difference."

He pushed his fingers through his hair and tugged on it. "You said she was your mother. Is this all some delusional way to convince yourself she's not dead?"

I leaned into him, my arms stiff by my sides. "She's not dead!"

"She's too old to be hooking."

"She could be a madame. One of the girls knew a woman named Claudia."

"That all you got?" He threw his hands up. "There's lots of hookers named Claudia." God, I hated his condescending tone.

"The girl who knew Claudia had been part of your father's stable."

He froze and stared at me with shock in his eyes. "Fuck."

"She told me about other girls in the same situation. I find those girls and rescue them."

He paced away and back again. "I asked you straight out. Tell me about the stalker, and you lied like a first-class liar. Told me you didn't know who it was. Meanwhile, you're putting yourself, my team, Thorne, Soledad, and the entire cast of the

Metropolitan Opera at a huge risk. So tell me now. Is my father targeting you?"

"No. I don't think it's your father."

"Who the fuck is it?"

I could lie to him. I could refuse to tell him. But Falcon had a way of getting to the truth eventually. "The girl who knew Claudia had been sold to a man named Ivan Sharshinbaev."

His brows drew together. "I've heard of him."

"You have?"

"Yes, Rogan's working on a case related to him kidnapping some girls and turning them into slaves. You involved in that?"

"All the girls I've rescued had ties to Ivan Sharshinbaev."

"Well, shit. You should've told me this. You can't withhold critical information like this. Jesus, Aida. You've got six bodies on the ground, and you're lying through your teeth to me, to the investigators? Why? Why don't you give this information to the people who need it most?"

"What can a bureaucracy do? He's invincible. He can't be extradited to face accusations of American laws. He's a king in his country. If the police get involved, they arrest the girls for prostitution. They won't take care of them like I do. No one has even gotten close to touching Ivan or any of his men. This way works. I'm having the most impact on the ground, really helping people. Not running some kind of investigation from an office. Not talking about ways to extradite him, and wasting time trying to find evidence that meets some impossible law defining sex trafficking. There is no evidence. It's lots of small transactions that look like prostitution but it isn't. It's human trafficking and it's hard as hell to prosecute, especially internationally. There is only the women sitting there crying. They are desperate to be rescued. They can't wait for the law to save them. They need people like me who are willing to take chances, break the laws, and fight for them."

He looked at me for a long time. His mind processing the information. "Feel like fucking you."

"Falcon..."

"Feel like making you moan."

"Wow. You're so in touch with your feelings." I just poured my heart out to him, trusted him with my darkest secret, and he busted out cro-magnon man wanting to fuck. "There anything more to you than your dick?"

"Yes."

"Like what? Because I don't see it. I see a cold-hearted machine who could look at that girl, listen to her weep, listen to me tell you the most important parts of my life, and all you can say is you want to fuck?"

He stalked toward me, a grin growing on his lips. He bent down and scooped my legs up below my ass and lifted me up.

He carried me to a chair and sat down, forcing me to straddle him, my knees bent into the chair. Big warm hands settled on my hips and his pretty blue eyes focused on me.

"You're sweet inside. Like a chocolate lava cake."

"I am not."

"You don't want the public to know you got a soft spot. You're compassionate. You're a fighter. And you're brave."

Oh, that caught me off guard. "Wow. Almost sounds like you like me."

His hand came up and brushed my cheeks with the backs of his fingers. "I like you. And I get it. I get the pain you feel for those women. I get you wanna make it right. I've rescued a lot of women from bad situations. Not all of them came out alive, but I get how it tears up their lives, makes you want to kill someone for the way they've been treated. But you gotta stop risking your life to save theirs. When they're burying you, the priest is gonna have a hard time explaining why the opera darling died at the hands of a pimp. And I'm not gonna sit through your funeral. I've been through a lot of them and yours is not one I wanna attend. I'm gonna die before you just so I don't have to suffer through the sadness of the day they put you in the ground."

Oh. Well. Wow. "Thank you... for saying that."

"Don't get me wrong. You're still a hot mess."

I slapped his chest. "Shut up." I finally had him talking and I wanted more. "Tell me about the women you've rescued."

"Nah."

"I wanna hear. You say you get it, but do you really?"

"I get it. First woman I rescued was Soledad. I was only sixteen, but I knew I had to help her. My father and Manuel tore her up so bad, she was losing it. Got her out of there. Feel good about that. She's happy now with a solid man at her side. Your mom ended up in the same situation, and I set up the escape. Saved you from a dark future. Signed up for the Army, rescued American hostages in Iraq, Afghanistan, and Syria. Helped my buddy Torrez get his woman out of Manuel's hands. Those are just a few. There were others."

"And what about the ones who didn't make it?"

He glanced out the window then back at me. "You wanna know? I'll tell you because you might learn from it and realize what kinda fire you're playing with." His hands squeezed my hips. "I told you about the wife Rogan had before the one he has now. He warned her not to follow him. She did. She got kidnapped and killed. We buried her. None of us ever got past it. Every time we see a woman like Isabella, we all remember the vivid details of Eden's death. She wasn't his soulmate, but losing her set us all on the path we're on now."

"You believe in soulmates?"

"The way Rogan loves Tessa, you got no choice. Those two were meant to be. For me? Nah. I control how I feel about everything so I won't let myself fall in love. Even if my soul-mate shows up and bewitches me like a snake charmer, I can resist because I got no dreams of it working out."

The floodgates had opened. Falcon was sharing. "What dreams do you have?"

"I don't dream. I plot. First plot is finding out more about Ivan and his network and looking into bringing him to justice. Second is my father. I let him live because I thought it would be fun. Seeing as he affected the girl you met and probably lots of others, I'm thinking he needs to have a come-to-Jesus moment."

"I dream," I said with a wry smile.

His hands ran up and down my sides. "I know you do. I bet you have nice dreams with lots of love and soulmates and destiny shit."

I tilted my head and thought about how to answer him. "Sometimes. I believe in love. I believe there's someone we're meant to love. It just takes time to find them. Our heart has to be ready for it and open to it. That hasn't happened for me yet."

His lips curled into a naughty smirk. "Hopefully it doesn't happen before our arrangement is over because your soul-mate might not appreciate my dick in your cunt."

I gasped and laughed. "Jesus, Falcon. So callous."

"Sayin' it like it is." His hand patted my thigh. "You find your soulmate, he has to wait for Ivan to die." He looked up at my hair and reached for it.

"So the arrangement is over when Ivan is taken down?" We were dancing around dangerous territory here.

"Yes." He twirled my hair around his finger.

I didn't like the casual way he implied he could stick to the arrangement. A huge part of me wanted him to feel sad it would end, but he showed no emotion. "And then you'll go after your father?"

"Most likely." He sounded very non-committal for a man who just said he preferred to plot over dream.

"And when he's dead?" I asked him.

He shrugged. "I don't know. Suppose I'll look up some hits and see who needs to die next."

I couldn't hide my frown. His future sounded bleak and depressing. "Well, that's lovely."

His hand moved to my neck, and his fingers twisted into my hair. "You want an extension of the arrangement? Can't live without the titanium cock?"

God, he was so cocksure! "No. You can come and go as you please. I have my own life to live." I turned my nose up and masked any emotion I was feeling. I wasn't giving that to him if he didn't want it.

"Okay, mi paloma. Gonna fuck you now."

Falcon was done talking. I knew it wouldn't last long. That was fine with me because sitting on his lap with his hands exploring had made me hot and bothered. "Mmm." I wiggled my hips, trying to get deeper into him.

He raised his hips and pressed his hard cock against my core, igniting a spark that sizzled from the back of my neck down to my toes.

"Yeah, she likes the titanium cock."

"Shut up and kiss me."

And he did. We made out on the chair for twenty minutes, just teasing like we did in the dressing room. His hands caressed every inch of my ass, including the crack. I pulled his shirt up and trailed my fingers over his hard skin. Beautiful. I scratched my fingers through the hair on his chest and pulled the shirt off to admire his shoulders.

He had me so turned on, I couldn't stand it anymore. I scooted to the floor, worked his pants open, and freed his cock. It stood strong and big in front of my face. I'd never seen one so big. Every penis I'd ever seen had been six inches or so and reasonable size. Falcon's cock dwarfed all those in both length and girth. My core ached thinking about how good it felt inside me, filling me up. His hand in my hair wrapped around my head and pushed down, encouraging me to suck it. With one hand braced on his knee and the other around the thick base of his cock, I slipped the swollen tip into my mouth.

His head fell back with a groan. The piercings added a whole secondary level of erotic stimulation for both of us, and I loved drawing the sharp, savage cries out of him.

Lord, he tasted incredible. Salty pre-come dripping from the tip. A musky scent coming from the hair at the base. A masculine man. Not a dancer or an actor. Falcon was the real thing.

The cold metal balls of his apa rubbed my tongue. His hand pushed down, forcing more of his bulging cock into my mouth. I opened wide to allow room for the piercings, but didn't move. I'd done this before, but each time I'd feared hurting him.

"Suck. Hard. It's okay."

I closed my lips tight and pulled back with a hard suck. He groaned louder, his hands digging into my hair, his legs dropping open wider. The beads played against my lips before popping out of my mouth.

"Fuuuck. You're gonna kill me."

"Mmm," I mumbled around his cock. I loved how he became so unhinged when I did this.

"Jesus, mi alma." *My soul.*

I wanted him to come in my mouth. Wanted to feel that explosion close up, smell it, make it happen, taste it and swallow it.

His hands reached under my armpits and pulled me off his dick. I stared down at the glistening wet shaft. "I want it."

"Gonna come inside you. Gonna fill you up. Want you to moan in my mouth. Yes?"

I stood up and bent to kiss him. "Yes."

He slid my pants and underwear over my hips. I stepped out of them. He lifted his hips, raising his big red cock like a flag as he took a condom from his wallet.

"Climb on up." He ripped the packet open with his teeth, one hand on my ass pulling me toward him. I spread my legs and straddled him, using my hands on his broad shoulders to steady me. On my tiptoes, I held my hips just above the tip of his condom-covered cock. When he pulled my neck down to kiss him, the tip of his dick brushed my skin. God, it felt good. So tempting and tasty and erotic. Everything with Falcon made me feel alive, sensual, and lucky. "Take it. It's yours. Take it all."

His hands drew my hips down, and we both groaned as he slipped inside. Each bead bumping and teasing me as I slid down.

He tugged my hair and forced my back to arch. He lifted my shirt, his mouth engulfed my nipple. His hand on my hip pumped me up and down on his dick. The thumb of his other hand slid over to my clit and swept it in lazy circles.

We moved slowly, enjoying each slide of skin on skin.

His hips jerked up, his hand in my hair pulled my mouth to his, and I released a long, rich, earth-shattering moan into his mouth. He grunted his approval, and my world erupted into one eternal climax.

He ended the kiss and looked down to watch us fucking. I panted into his ear as he dragged out my orgasm, rolling it right into the genesis of another one.

"Fuck yeah. Fucking A. Fuck me. Yeah." The low scratchy whisper of his words and our skin slapping together vibrated loud in my ear. The sounds of total unleashed, raw sex.

He squeezed my hips tight and constrained me in place as he pumped into me from below. He seated himself deep and groaned, his dick reaching far inside me. I watched his stunning face as he came. All Falcon's intensity jetted out of him. His mouth opened, the veins in his neck popped, and a low drawn-out growl emerged from deep in his throat.

A few more slow pumps and his breathing calmed. I sighed and rested my forehead on his shoulder.

His hand reached for my chin and his thumb and forefinger drew me in for a scorching, wet kiss. God, I could kiss Falcon forever. I could stay like this with his giant cock filling me, watching his face go slack, smelling his strong scent. Just please let me stay like this forever.

I opened my eyes to see his had changed. They looked at me differently. With affection, respect, and God, it looked like it could be love. He'd just told me he didn't believe in love, but that kiss spelled it out in neon pink cursive letters. *Love.*

But he'd said he could never feel love. He wouldn't allow it. We'd agreed to sex. We'd decided no attachments. Cold panic drenched me like I'd fallen naked into the snow. I pulled away and tried to get up but his heavy forearm wrapped around my waist and hauled me down. "Stay." He lifted his chin and the warmth of his breath tickled my ear. "Stay," he repeated.

I flopped limply back onto his massive frame. Fine. Let him stay inside me and hold me. For now, in the present, I had this magnificent moment. Falcon under me, begging me to stay.

Tomorrow and yesterday could wait. For now, I could stay.

As we cuddled and our bodies cooled, he kept both arms tight around my back, pressing my boobs into his chest. His arms loosened, and he sucked in a big breath of air. He blew it out slowly. "Your vigilante days are over."

"But..."

"We'll come up with a plan, but no more acting alone. It's too dangerous."

The desperation in his command made me pause. He often became withdrawn and remorseful after sex, but this time he remained connected emotionally. He turned off his natural instinct to shut down, and I respected that gesture. I didn't like the idea of giving up on the rescues, but I had to honor his fervid pleas. I'd pretty much give him anything he wanted at this point.

"Okay," I whispered.

He grinned and tucked his forehead into my neck.

Chapter 16

———

FALCON INSISTED WE fly to Los Angeles early. Rehearsals for the musical adaptation of Aida didn't begin for another week, and yet he booked the flight, rented a mansion in Beverly Hills, and cancelled all excursions until the "security had been optimized."

He said we could manage risks better in a house than a hotel. Gaspar knew the director and had also arranged a role for Thorne. He moved into the Beverly Hills mansion with us.

For the first week, Falcon, Blaze, and Diesel set up their cameras and built a fortress of bulletproof windows and doors.

While they were "optimizing," Thorne and I lounged by the pool. I loved New York. The city hummed with excitement, people walked fast, always in a hurry. The laid back vibe of Hollywood and the relaxing sunshine in California also sat well with me and helped calm my nerves.

The mansion had a music room with a piano, a small platform that acted as a stage, and some recording and audio equipment. My vocal coach met with me once, but most of my time was spent with Thorne. It was a glorious week. I didn't forget my worries, but my body thanked me for the down time and reduced stress.

Falcon worked all day, at least I assumed he was working, but I rarely saw him except for brief moments in the kitchen for meals. He spent his evenings in the gym with one of the guys; I may have spied on him a little. After his shower, he'd join me in bed for sex and sleep. He still did his thing where he got out of the bed and sulked in a chair, but he was returning to me more quickly this week.

Tonight he came into the kitchen as I was flipping my lasagna casserole onto a serving platter.

He stared at it with his eyebrows high. "What's that?"

I had to admit the round pile of baked noodles looked odd on the plate. "It's dome lasagna. Traditional lasagna in a bowl. You serve it upside down."

He looked at me then at the platter again. "You cook?"

"Of course I cook. I'm a regular person just like anyone else. I've always loved lasagna and this recipe makes it special."

The curious look on his face triggered a memory. We'd stopped at an Italian restaurant on the drive to New Jersey when he was eighteen and I was fifteen. I'd been brave and ordered lasagna because the picture looked so delicious. That was when I first fell in love with it. Since then, it'd been my biggest weakness, so I only made it for special occasions like this one, where I was locked up in a house and couldn't go out to eat.

I cut him a piece shaped like a pie. "Try it." The cheese and tomato sauce had blended magically into steaming layers of sin. The decadent smell of baked lasagna filled the kitchen.

He took the plate and fork I offered and brought a bite to his mouth. His eyes widened and he chewed and swallowed with an appreciative smile. "Damn, woman. That is excellent. Never would have guessed you could cook."

"I have many hidden talents," I said with a cheeky grin.

"True." He winked at me and devoured the rest of his piece in a few manly bites. He dropped his empty dish and his fork in the sink and walked to the hallway. "Looking forward to tasting more of your hidden talents tonight," he threw back as he left the kitchen.

FALCON WOKE ME UP WITH his mouth between my legs. I had my first orgasm before becoming fully conscious. We had mind blowing sex, me on my knees, him pressed up to my backside. His fingers brought me through another orgasm before he grunted into my neck, and his hand around my belly slammed me down hard on his cock. My head fell back onto his shoulder, and he caressed my breasts over my silk nightgown.

"Mornin'," his gravelly voice rasped in my ear.

"Mmm. Lovely morning." He folded us at the waist and somehow managed to get us lying side by side without losing our connection. "What a way to wake up." Blissed out, happy from lots of great sex, held safe in the massive arms of a sexy guy.

He kissed my neck and ran his hand up and down my side. He started to get hard again inside me. Maybe he wanted to go another round. I'd be up for it, but I felt the loss of him as he pulled out. "Gotta go to Boston."

My warm fuzzies turned into cold empty fizzles. "Why?"

"Gonna meet with Rogan and a couple guys with dirt on Ivan."

"Oh."

"See what they've got. Make plans to end this."

I turned in his arms and looked him in the eye. "Killing Ivan won't save the girls he's already sold. There's thousands of pimps in his network."

He stood and stared down at me. "I know that, but taking him out is key to stopping the flow of girls into the system. The abductions end if there's no one to fund them."

"It's a start."

His nostrils flared as he scowled. "Jesus. Killing the king of a small country is not a start. It's the end. You know how hard it's going to be to get to him? The logistics and legal implications alone are impossible."

"That's what I'm saying. There's no time to stop it at the top. We have to work from the street level. Every woman I rescue is required to volunteer for the shelter. I have thousands of advocates ready to help."

"We," he pointed at me, "don't have to do anything. You and those women are not working the street anymore."

Who was he to dictate to me that I should give up all my hard work? I was making a difference. What was he doing? "What about the girls I haven't saved yet? What about their families who are searching for them?"

"You are a fucking singer. Not God. You can't solve the problem of human trafficking. It's huge. Millions of women all over the world. The best we can do is get rid of Ivan and disrupt his network. Now, you wanna give me shit about that, I'll skip it and get back to killing my own assholes. I don't mind dropping this scam. Would be much more fulfilling to kill my father right now than spend months seeking out the corrupt king of some former Russian country."

Uh oh. Now I'd pissed him off so bad he wanted to give up on Ivan. I had to be nice if I wanted his help.

"No. Please don't give up on me. Whatever you can do, I appreciate. Taking Ivan down would be a huge win."

"Fine. I'll see what I can do about Ivan if you promise to stop the vigilante crap."

"I already said I would."

"But I don't trust you, and I'm leaving. Won't be able to keep an eye on you."

There it was. He didn't trust me. He thought he needed to babysit me.

"I promise no more rescues. I have to concentrate on this performance anyway."

"Good." He kept staring at me. Both of us naked. He'd won. I'd agreed to everything he'd said and he still held onto his anger.

"So you'll be gone for a long time?" I asked to change the subject.

"Possibly. Blaze will take over your security detail. Rogan is sending two guys to replace me here."

He'd already made arrangements? He certainly didn't act like he was planning to leave last night when he'd flirted with me over lasagna and definitely not just now as we'd had sex. "It takes two men to replace you?"

"I've been giving you special treatment. Normal bodyguards get some down time." I never asked him to treat me differently than anyone else.

"I see. Well, goodbye then." I turned away from him, raising my shoulder to hide my face.

He stayed quiet for a minute. His gaze burned into my back. I wanted to scream *get out* but I held my tongue.

Finally he spoke. "You're not getting attached, are you?" The acid in his voice scratched my skin like a wire broom across my back. "It's an arrangement. Temporary."

God, his tone implied I was a weakling out of control.

"Of course not." Asshole. That's what this was about? He was afraid I was getting attached?

I rolled over to watch him stomp naked to the bathroom. The toilet flushed and he came back, pulling up his pants. His beautiful dick flipped inside as he zipped up. "This is why I never do this. I never fuck the same woman twice. Never fuck available women. They get attached. Women are not capable of having sex without adding all kinds of false emotion to it. They make shit up that isn't there."

I may have been doing that. His touch seemed so affectionate. He acted like he was into me. But I blew it. Again. Got involved with a self-centered jerk who would break my heart. I was safer with Thorne and my dildos. "Fuck you, Falcon."

"Admit it. You've lost control. You're having dreams about you and me pledging eternal love and making babies." He said *babies* with a sneer. I didn't like this ugly side of Falcon. He was better when he stayed silent and brooding.

"I'm not. I'm dreaming of my new show and winning awards for my work. The last thing I want is to get knocked up by some dickhead douchenozzle."

His jaw clenched, but his eyes laughed at my name calling. Screw him.

"Good." He grabbed his shirt and yanked it over his head. "Don't dream about me. Don't get ideas. It's not gonna happen."

I'd had enough. I sat up in bed, holding the sheet over my chest. "I am Aida Soltari." I used my superior diva voice. "Solitary. No stupid man to bring me down or hold me back. I have always been alone."

He propped his hands on his hips and popped one knee out. "You are Magdalena Esperanza. A fake and a manipulator."

Oh really? Fucking really? He wanted to fight? "You are Primitivo de la Cruz. Serial killer." I spat the last two words at him.

His eyes flashed and he leaned in, planting his fists in the bed on either side of me. "Daughter of a whore and a john."

Oh now. Fuck him. I would not bend to his insults. I had my own to retort. "First son of a genocidal narco boss."

He flinched and backed away from me. His teeth came out and bit his lower lip. His hands twitched. He looked like his father then. The machismo dictator of Northern Mexico that slaughtered innocent people without remorse.

Falcon forced his arms back with a growl. I raised my chin. Fine. Let him hit me. See how he liked the consequences. I'd report him for abuse and have him arrested for murdering Manuel.

His eyes narrowed on me. "Change in plans. I'm not going after Ivan for you. I'm off this case and not coming back."

Oh, who was manipulating now? He knew I couldn't take down Ivan without him. "Who cares? You couldn't even find my mother! It took you twenty-two years to kill Manuel. I don't have the time to wait for you to get to Ivan." A low blow, but he'd pushed me over the edge.

His face turned red, and his eyes glinted. "Has anything happened to you since I've been on this case?"

Well, not really. "Nothing except for the threatening email."

"Exactly. I know what I'm doing. Do not doubt me."

He'd said that before. He hated being questioned, but he'd pissed me off so I kept fighting. "It's a mere coincidence nothing happened in the time you were here."

He nodded his head, and the heat left his eyes. Only cold dark hardness remained. "Right. Then it'll also be a coincidence when I'm gone and you get your delusional head blown off."

He turned and stuffed his gun in his hip holster.

"Fine. Leave. I don't care. But you are going to miss me."

He laughed and marched to the door.

"I'm not the one getting attached, Falcon. Think about it. Why are you really huffing and puffing around the room?"

He sneered at me. "Goodbye, Aida."

"You're breaking your own heart."

"I don't have a heart." He slammed the door behind him with a big gust of air.

Oh my God. Why did I let him in my life? In my bed? Always the fool. Always the loser. Always solitary.

The tears pricked the back of my eyelids. No. I wouldn't shed a tear for him. It was my own fault. I trusted him knowing who he was. He grew up in a ruthless crime family. He had no respect for human life or women's dignity. I'd never make that mistake again.

I lasted about a minute. The dust settled. The wind blew and rattled the windows. I grabbed my pillow and cried.

Never again. Never trust a man again.

Especially not Primitivo de la Cruz.

Chapter 17

———

FALCON

Sitting on my Harley, outside a motel in Austin, Texas, I watched her belt out "Ya Te Olividé" on a late night talk show. I'd watched it at least thirty times already.

She wore a long black and white dress with tight fabric that glistened and wrapped up her curves like snakeskin. A huge slit up the side revealed her leg to the top of her sensuous thigh.

The tiny black triangle of her thong showed through her dress when the light hit it from behind. Every time. Every time she went on stage, that triangle showed through. She had to know. She had to be doing it on purpose.

The dress covered her nipples and tied around her neck, but side-boob was on full display. No bra, her breasts looked fantastic.

The musical in Los Angeles wrapped up last night. After this late night performance, she had a break until her next gig at the Met. She had chosen to stay in the house in LA with Thorne until she had to leave. She liked it there. Of course she did. Hollywood was a utopian make believe where she could pretend her problems didn't exist.

Since no physical threats had appeared since we'd been there, I'd allowed it.

Thick black eyeliner and silver makeup around her eyes made her look vulnerable and on the verge of tears. But as the song built, she grew strong and confident. Long earrings swaying. Her mouth open wide like when she blew me. Hot as hell. A woman scorned. No one else could own that song like her. She sold it, and the audience ate it up. She strutted her ass around the stage like a queen, her right fist up above her head, left hand gripping the microphone. Thorne's ring shone on her finger.

Her gaze drilled in on the camera.

At me.

I've already forgotten you.

With the last note, her voice broke in a weak whisper. She dropped her head, bangs falling into her face. Despair eating her up.

Her act.

Or was it?

After the way I left it, I had to own it. I caused her this pain. I hit her where it hurts the most. I used her past against her as a weapon. That made me a bastard.

Even though I'd warned her, a woman like her could never have sex without emotion. No. Only a mountain of intense passion and desire. She gave it to me every time—even the first time—like she loved me. Or she wanted to.

Fuck me if I didn't get off on it.

But I let it go too far. I had to leave before it got messy, but it was a tough pill to swallow watching her sing a song to me while she stood there crying, half naked on stage.

A text came in on my burner phone. My father. He'd contacted me via Rogan a week ago.

El diablo: Tomorrow 8pm Tunnel 6

My father had seen me at the Latin Choice Awards with Aida. He hadn't said whether he'd recognized her or not. He'd only said he'd seen me and wanted a meet.

Now he'd set the time and place. Tomorrow night in the tunnels I helped him to dig. Men had died in those tunnels from lack of oxygen or the walls caving in. They'd also died by execution. If Guillermo de la Cruz took you down into the tunnels, say goodbye to your momma because you weren't coming back

I wasn't sure what his motives were, but I could guess. He wanted his money back.

If he killed me, he'd never get it.

If he let me live, he'd never get it.

But I took the meet anyway.

Time to reunite with dear old Dad.

———————————

IN ONE HAND, I CARRIED a flashlight. In the other, my Sig.

Helix tracked me in the shadows. I brought him as my back-up because I couldn't ask Rogan to provide a man to follow me into the belly of the whale. Helix was a bounty hunter who trailed Torrez awhile back. Somewhere along the line, he became an ally, so I chose him to go with me tonight.

As I bent under low sections of tunnel six, the air became thin. I stopped a few meters away from four men I once knew. Not anymore.

My father, two of my brothers, and my cousin. The first time we'd been face-to-face in twenty-two years.

He'd brought them to challenge me. Daring me to kill my own family like I did the night I'd betrayed him. They also stood as a symbol of the family I lost. They still had each other while I had nothing. I chose to walk away.

I stood by that decision. I'd rather be alone than be part of evil.

My brothers' faces had aged poorly. Wrinkles, hunched backs. They held new rifles in their grip. Not the old AK-47s we learned to fight with as children.

"I'm surprised you showed up, Primitivo." My father spoke his first words to my face since I was eighteen years old. The last ones had been the order to kill Manuel's women. The order I did not follow. His face had fallen and sagged. His belly had grown rounder, but his eyes had not changed. Cold and black.

"Why would I not?"

"You aren't afraid I will exact revenge for the killings of your brother, Manuel, and all the men you've been taking out over the years?"

Ah, so he did know it was me. "No idea what you're talking about."

"Why did you come?" he asked.

Why did I come? Because I'd been fighting the same quixotic battle for far too long. Time for a change. Either he died or I died, but the vendetta would end. "I had nothing else to do. What do you want?"

"I want Claudia."

I had expected him to say money. I assumed he knew I had stolen his fortune. When Manuel died, his last source of income would have dried up. He had to be hurting.

Claudia's name spoken by him shocked me and made my skin crawl. "Claudia? I don't know where she is. I thought Manuel had her."

"Manuel sold her years ago."

"To who?"

"A Russian. Don't know his name."

"I'm sure you don't."

"I saw you with her daughter on TV. Magdalena is a famous singer."

Anger roiled in my gut and I spoke through clenched teeth. "Keep your hands off her."

"If Claudia is dead, Lena is all I have left of her."

Fuck no. This was not happening. "Magdalena is not your daughter. Claudia came to Nuevo Laredo with her. You can't be the father."

"No, but I loved her. And I loved her girl like the daughter I never had."

"Bullshit. The way you treated Claudia, you didn't love her and you would've done the same to Magdalena."

"Please, Tivo. I'd like to see Lena."

"No way in hell." And don't fucking call her Lena.

"I want to make amends with her."

No. He knew she had money as a celebrity and he wanted it. I had to stop this now. Even if it meant confessing to my father. "If you stay away from her, I'll give you all your money back."

His eyes blew wide and a smirk grew on his thin lips. "My money? You took it from me? I thought it might have been you, but I told myself my oldest son would never betray me like that. Now you confirm you are a traitor. God will strike you down."

"Stay away from Magdalena, and I'll wire it to you in chunks."

His empty hands came forward and pleaded with me. "You must believe I wanted to meet Lena and I wanted to make amends."

"I don't give a shit what you say you want. This is what I'm offering. You stay away from her and you die a rich man. My brothers and cousin behind you will get the money when you die."

He squinted and looked behind me in the tunnel. "How can I trust you?"

"You can't. Chance you take."

His eyes held doubt and mistrust. All we'd ever had between us.

He turned to speak to my brothers and my cousin. After a minute, they broke and faced me. They smirked and their eyes glowed. Oh shit.

"We don't make deals with traitors," my father said with his chin raised.

"Bullshit." He'd teamed up with Manuel. Traitors make vicious soldiers. But I knew where he was going with this.

"If you fight your brothers and your cousin, your betrayal is not forgotten. You killed Oscar and robbed from your family. This does not erase anything. But you have paid your penance, we will call a truce."

A man like him never honored a truce if it didn't meet his agenda. "For the rest of her life, you never come near Magdalena. I see your face, catch even a scent of any one of you, the money stops and I come back and kill you all." I pegged each of my brothers and my cousin with my gaze. Before they exacted their unfair penance on me, they needed to see the threat in my eyes. "Keep your word or die at my hands."

"If you survive, Primitivo, we have a deal." My father's voice sounded genuinely sad. I knew better than to fall for it.

My training kicked in automatically. Multiple attackers. If you can't run, separate and disable one at a time. No hesitation. Short, quick, efficient punches.

Adrenaline zipped through my every vein like burning whiskey. I could take them all on and win. They may have me outnumbered, but they never advanced beyond street fighting. I could take them with cunning and resourcefulness.

My muscles hummed, guard came up, and chin tilted down. Let's go.

My father nodded at his second oldest, Hugo.

I didn't see him as my closest younger brother. I only saw a threat to be neutralized. "C'mon, asshole."

I dropped into a shoulder roll and nailed him with a fierce groin kick. He doubled over in pain.

The other two came at me as I popped up. I maneuvered one into a headlock and lined them up using the first one as a shield. I kneed Juan Carlo in the face, but Alex caught my foot and twisted, forcing me to the ground.

He jumped on top of me. We wrestled for a second, but I couldn't shake him. When Juan Carlo and Hugo recovered and joined Alex on top of me, all I could do was duck and cover and pray like fuck the fight had taken some of their energy. But I knew better. These guys would kick me all night if my father allowed it.

"Traitor!" Pointed boots rammed into my ribs over and over. Punches slammed my face. My head spun and the bitter taste of blood pooled on my tongue.

Sharp pain hit my legs, back, arms. Shit. Would they ever stop?

I'd be sore for weeks, but if this beating kept my father off Aida's path, I'd take ten more.

"Enough," my father finally called.

They left me on the dirt floor, spitting blood, but not dead.

No never dead.

The falcon rose above.

The last thing I tasted was dirt mixed with blood before the world went black.

I WOKE UP TO SEARING pain. Freezing cold and burning hot on my ribs. Throbbing fire in my legs. An exploded grenade in my head. Blood came back on my fingers when I touched my face.

"The one on your eye needs a bandage."

I groaned and Helix laughed.

"You got me out of there?" My swollen tongue tasted like I ate a tire.

"Carried you out. Heavy mother fucker."

"Thank you."

One eye swollen shut, I peeked through the other one to survey the damage. A few cuts on my arms, ice bags on my stomach. Blood on my shirt.

Fuck. Was this worth it? Was anything worth feeling like a fucking smashed pumpkin with the pulp hanging out? Yeah. If my father stayed the fuck away from Aida, it would be worth it. Last thing she needed in her life was a visit from her past. Including me. We both needed to leave her the fuck alone.

Helix checked his phone, reminding me I hadn't checked mine. My shoulders and ribs screamed as I twisted to pull it out of my pocket.

Fucking ten missed calls. Twenty messages.

Blaze, Rogan, Dallas. None from Diesel.

Fuck. Fuck. Fuck.

Without reading shit, I called Blaze. I'd warned him. I'd told him no one gets to her. If he'd fucked up...

"Falc." His voice was tight and stressed.

"Talk."

"Two men. One shooter. From a boat. The Beach House restaurant in Malibu."

Holy fucking shit. "Was she hit?"

"No."

My lungs ached as I blew out a relieved breath. "Thank fuck." Thank God nothing happened to her.

"But Gaspar Evaristo took a bullet for her."

Oh shit. "Fatal?"

"He's at Santa Monica Medical Center. Critical condition. His spine."

"Fuck." She loved Gaspar like a father. The world famous Gaspar Dominquez had been shot by hitmen out after Aida. Shit. This just went global.

"Yeah. Diesel's there too. Three gunshot wounds. Head, arms."

Oh man. I had one straw left and he just snapped it. My brothers who shared my blood could rot in hell, but Diesel and I were brothers to the core. No one shot at him and lived. "Where are you now?"

"I'm with Aida at LA County Sheriff's Department."

"Why the fuck is she at the sheriff's department?"

"They took her in as a suspect. Three terrorist acts involving her in one year."

"Fuck."

"She lost it when she saw Gaspar bleeding on top of her. She screamed. Wouldn't calm down. Sheriffs cuffed her and drove her downtown."

"Shit."

"They questioned me too. Released me within an hour.

"Good."

"I'm not sure the threat is neutralized. I asked Thorne to watch over Gaspar until more men arrive. I need to get back to Diesel. His fucking head, Falc. I need to get back there."

"No one is with him?"

"No."

"Jesus Christ."

What a clusterfuck.

A vision of Aida in a holding cell came vividly to my mind. She was hunched forward in a chair. Heaving. Weeping. Scared and alone after interrogators worked her over as her father figure lay fighting for his life in a hospital.

"You call Dallas?"

"Dallas and Rogan are flying in tomorrow. Ruger and Oz were in New York prepping for a gig she has on her schedule. They're coming here too."

"I'm on the next plane."

Helix gave me a confused look. I was in no condition to travel, but I needed to get there right away.

"I'm sorry, Falc." Blaze went on. "We vetted the restaurant, but didn't think anyone would approach by boat. After the first shot, Gaspar threw himself on Aida. Then fucking Diesel tried to run a distraction and swam toward the shooter. It worked. He turned on Diesel, and I dragged Gaspar and Aida behind a rock. After that, I couldn't get a lock on the boat. I finally nailed him when he stopped to reload. They took off. No idea who they were."

"Jesus, D is crazy."

"Yeah. I'm worried as fuck. But couldn't leave Aida."

"Thanks for sticking with her. Hold it together till I get there. Five hours tops."

I hung up and stared at Helix. I needed his help.

"What's up?" he asked.

"Can you watch my gun for me while I fly to California?"

His brow drew tight as he frowned at me. "What the fuck?"

"I need to catch an emergency domestic flight. Take care of my Sig for me."

"Why?"

Dude. Every word hurt, I needed him to play along. "I'm fond of it, alright? I'll hook up with you another time to reclaim it."

He took the Sig from me and turned it over in his hand. "You trust me with this?"

"Sure." As much as two hitmen could trust each other. "It's my favorite. I don't have time to store it. You got it, or we gonna waste more time talking about it?"

"I got it." He stuffed it in his waistband behind his back.

"Now help me get to an airport."

"Probably need to wash the blood off first."

"Shit. That's gonna hurt."

Chapter 18

AN HOUR INTO THE FLIGHT to Los Angeles, the vision haunted me. Aida sobbing in a jail cell. Scared, worried, alone, and in shock. Her beautiful dark hair and warm skin all wrong against the concrete walls.

I never should've left her.

Rogan picked up my call on the first ring. "Where the fuck have you been?" He knew it would take something pretty strong to keep me from her when she needed me.

"You don't want to know." I coughed and tried to hide the blood from the view of the stewardesses, but they'd been giving me inquisitive looks since I sat down. I looked like death walking, and I understood their fear. I'd be scared too if I saw me.

"You alright?" Rogan asked.

"I'll survive. I need a favor."

"I'm flying out to LA at 0800."

"Aida's being held for questioning at LASD. I want her released pronto. Call someone."

"Who did you have in mind?"

"Fuck. Anyone. Call Lachlan and have him pull some federal bullshit? Dallas or Torrez got business connections in LA? Or your mom? Shit. Call in a favor with Brightman, but I need her out of there right away."

He didn't hesitate. "On it." Any time of day, Rogan always came through for me. Hopefully he could pull this one off too.

"I'm enroute to LAX. ETA three hours. I never shoulda left her."

"Blaze is with her," he said, trying to placate me.

"You think I trust Blaze? His mind is at that hospital with Diesel and you know it. She's totally vulnerable."

"She's in custody. She should be safe there." He kept his voice calm and that pissed me off. Did he not see the danger here?

"What if Sharshinbaev has the cops on his payroll and they arrested her so they could get her alone?" I had to fight to keep my voice down in the plane.

"Not plausible. You're fucked in the head, Falc. She's safe."

What the fuck did he know? Why was he being so damn aloof? "She's not safe until she's in my arms alive. Not bleeding to death on the helo floor."

He paused a long time.

Oh shit. I'd said the wrong fucking thing. Eden died on the floor of the helo in Afghanistan after we failed to rescue her in time.

"This is different." His voice was calm, but raspy. "She's in custody at the sheriff's department. She hasn't been captured. She will survive."

"Right."

"Past was ugly, man. Gotta let it go."

"Right." Took a minute for his words to penetrate the haze of my battered brain. "Assuming she's safe, she's gotta be terrified. She's been through a shooting, and now they're holding her in a cell."

He snickered. "You care about her."

Leave it to Rogan to nail me on that. I shook my head, but it hurt so I stopped. Enough of this talking about emotions crap. "I want Sharshinbaev. Tell Torrez and Zook to meet us in Cali for a strategy session." I had shared Aida's connection to Ivan, but we'd decided not to go to Veranistaad. Rogan had convinced me to wait for the justice system to take its course. That had all changed today.

"Let's get everyone stabilized first." He was again being logical in the face of my utter frustration.

"Right."

"You okay? You sound like shit."

"Got in a fight. I'm a little beat up."

"Take care of yourself, Falc. I'll be there in the morning."

"Okay."

"Good luck, man."

"Yeah."

MY EXPRESS RENTAL CAR waited for me at LAX. No traffic at two in the morning, so I made the forty minute trip to the station in twenty.

Blaze met me outside and stared at the swelling on my face. "What the fuck happened to you?"

I touched the bandage over my eye to make sure it wasn't leaking again. "Rough flight. What's the status?"

"They're waiting for a lawyer to call." The stress of the day showed in the wrinkles on his face and the tight clench of his jaw.

"No lawyers up this time of night."

"Yeah." His gaze shot to the door, scanned the street, back to me, and the door again.

"Go to him," I said. He was of no use to me here, and someone needed to be with Diesel.

His eyebrows lifted. "You sure?"

"I got her. You go. Check on Gaspar and Thorne too. We'll meet up at the mansion when Rogan arrives."

"Thank you, Falc." He took three steps backward. "You alright?" He pointed to my face.

"Yeah. Go."

He ran down the sidewalk and around the side of the building.

I knocked and a guard came to the door of the station. "You got a reason to be here?" The short middle-aged guard put his hands on his belt and peered up at me. I could see his eyes judging me. Mexican, thug.

"Aida Soltari," I said, throwing her name like a weapon.

He opened the door and let me in.

"I'm here to take Aida Soltari home."

His bald head shined in the overhead lights as he typed in the computer.

"It says we're waiting to hear from her lawyer. She's here till morning." He gave me a smug grin.

"Fuck." I paced away, trying to lock it down. "Do you know who she is?"

"I don't care who she is. I'm following orders."

"Jesus Christ. She's a fucking celebrity being stalked by terrorists."

He shook his head.

"Call your fucking captain and tell him Gaspar Evaristo has been shot, and you're holding his daughter for questioning while he is dying in the hospital. Tell him she's unstable and needs care, and I'm here to provide it."

"Have a seat."

I stared at him. "I'll give you five minutes to get your supervisor on the phone and release her, or I'm going to call every fucking press agency in Hollywood and tell them you've locked up Aida Soltari without cause. She's the victim here. Not the suspect."

As we stared at each other, his phone rang and mine buzzed.

Rogan: Brightman made some calls.

Thank fuck Rogan had the Secretary of State in his back pocket. The woman would do anything for him. Even call Los Angeles in the early morning hours.

The guard coughed and hung up the phone. "This way." He grabbed a set of keys from his desk and walked down the hallway.

Pain from the cuts, scrapes, and bruises disappeared as he led me back to the holding cell.

I held back the urge to break through the white door with a small glass panel in it. I wanted to burst in, grab her, and carry her out of this place.

No. That would scare her.

My appearance alone would frighten her.

Funny how I laughed at Thorne and Soledad for coddling her, and here I was worrying about how my beat-up face would scare her.

She didn't look up as the guard opened the door. She matched the vision I'd had but worse. I didn't imagine her in a blood-stained white sundress. I didn't imagine her painted toes and pink sandals. She looked plucked from her glamorous life and forced into the cold harsh world of reality.

Her head bent over her knees, hair falling to the floor, hands over her face, shaking. Lost and alone like the fifteen-year-old Magdalena.

The guard raised an eyebrow in question.

"Give us a minute."

He nodded and closed the door.

"Aida." My voice scratched.

She peeked up, her face drawn, eyes smeared and red, lips quivering. Everything I never wanted for her. Exactly what I'd worked so hard to protect her from.

Her eyes took me in for several seconds. "Oh my God." She blinked a few times, coming out of herself to see me. "Oh my God!"

She stood and came to me. Her shaking hands touched my temple near the wound. I grabbed her hand to stop her.

"Did they do this to you?"

"No. No. Don't worry."

"Who did this to you?" Her other hand came up and patted my cheek. Her fingers grew frantic as they checked my shoulders and arms.

"You're bleeding." She lifted my shirt. Angry bruises marked my torso. "You're black and blue all over." Panic grew in her voice.

"Let's get you out of here."

"Who did this to you?" She ignored me. "Who did this to you?" she repeated with fire growing in her eyes.

"Babe."

Her hands clenched and she screeched, "Who did this to you!"

Fuck. I had to tell her or she'd think the worst. "My father had my brothers and my cousin dole out some justice."

"What?" She clawed at her face, and her lips turned down. "Your father? Your brothers... I- I can't handle this. It's too much."

"It's okay. I can handle it all." I opened my arms. She stepped closer and pressed her forehead into my chest with a whimper. I held her and spoke to her in Spanish like she had spoken to a frightened Isabella. "I've got you. You're safe. It will all be okay, mi paloma. I'm here."

"Gaspar..."

"He survived. He's in the hospital. I'll take you to him in the morning. You need sleep first."

She looked up at me and I wanted to kiss away the despair there. "Can't we go now?"

"No. You'll be safer at the house. I've got a team arriving in the morning, and we'll arrange for you to see Gaspar."

"Okay."

She tucked her head again and cried. "We were having lunch. He was fine. Sitting right next to me."

"I know."

"I heard popping sounds and he fell on me. I thought he'd fallen over. Then I saw the blood."

"He saved your life."

She whimpered.

"Let's get you home."

"But Diesel."

"He's at the hospital too. Blaze is with him. We'll check on him tomorrow too."

"I'm so scared."

"You're safe now. Deep breaths."

I let her cry it out. Took her tears on my shirt. Told myself I'd never do it, but if it helped her get through this, I'd take it.

"We got this. Let's go." Keeping her close under my arm, I guided her out the door and back to the front of the station. The guard handed me her bag and papers, and we made our way to my rental car.

I had my Aida back. We were both battered and weary, but I had my girl in my arms. Alive and safe.

Chapter 19

AIDA

Sunlight beaming through the windows of my idyllic Los Angeles mansion woke me from a restless sleep. Peeking from under my palms on my eyes, the clock said eleven a.m.

God, please let yesterday have been a dream. No one shot Gaspar or Diesel. The sheriffs didn't bring me in and question me.

And most of all, Falcon didn't show up at the station with a gash over his eye and hideous bruises staining his beautiful skin.

In the bathroom, my bloody clothes laying in the trash taunted me.

I couldn't deny it.

Yesterday happened, and a difficult day loomed in front of me.

I checked my phone for word from Gaspar's wife, Marcella.

Nothing.

I texted her.

Me: How is he this morning?

A few minutes passed before she responded.

Marcella: He's stable. We are waiting for him to wake up.

Me: I'll be there as soon as I can.

I had worn a white silk nightgown to bed last night. I found my favorite robe, given to me by one of my idols, an Italian soprano who sang Aida before me. Like slipping on a piece of art, the black, white, and red roses wrapped me in luxurious silk and provided the illusion of comfort in this chaos. In a rush, I tied it at my waist, and added red house shoes with a low heel.

I washed my face and added my eyes and lips before seeking out Falcon.

For a guy who drove a stake through my heart two months ago, he came through for me last night like a warrior. Even though he'd obviously been through a trauma with his father and family—one I dreaded asking the details about—he'd shown up and sprung me from the hell of the holding cell at the sheriff's office.

When we got home, we'd stripped off our clothes and showered in silence, both of us too exhausted to talk.

We'd put on sleep clothes and fell into bed, but I'd gotten up and brought him two capsules of acetaminophen. He downed them without taking the water I offered and tugged me into bed with him. For the first time ever, Falcon and I slept together without having sex. He even fell asleep before

I did. I watched him in the dark before I drifted off, worried about his injuries and the story behind them.

I liked that in an emergency, Falcon could bury all our differences, but I had no idea how he'd react to me today.

Despite my uncertainty about where I stood with Falcon, I needed to find him as soon as possible. Gaspar struggled for his life in a hospital bed with no one but his wife by his side. I needed to see Diesel too to make sure he would be okay.

I found Falcon in the dining room with four other men. Peeking around the corner, I only recognized Rogan. The other three must've been part of the team he mentioned last night. I paused in the doorway to eavesdrop, but they stopped talking, and five pairs of eyes appraised me in my robe.

Great job, Aida. You're wearing a slinky robe, with no bra, in front of a bunch of very macho, very buff guys.

My voice stuck in my throat. "I'd like to go see Gaspar. And, uh, Diesel."

Falcon coughed and stood from the table. His brow furrowed as he walked to me with his head tipped down and one hand over his stomach. He looked better today in a fresh pair of black cargo pants and a maroon waffle Henley, but he limped like walking caused him pain. His eye still didn't open fully, and his face was tired. "Give me a minute, mi paloma, and I'll take you to the hospital."

Oh well, that was sweeter than what I expected. "What're you guys talking about?" I whispered.

"Nothing."

"I want to know." I leaned to the side to see them sitting in silence. Two of them with eyes on me, Rogan and the other guy looking down at their laptops. "Did you tell them about Ivan?"

He glanced over his shoulder, and the two who were watching us looked away. "We're going after him."

"You're going to kill him?"

He held up a finger and touched my lips. "Shh. He shot Gaspar Evaristo and a member of my team. He's toast."

Oh my goodness, they were planning a murder! "I want to know everything."

"No." He said it curtly and condescending.

"I want to rescue more girls."

"No," he repeated more firmly, no room for discussion.

"Screw you, Falcon." The same fight we had weeks ago. He hadn't changed his stance at all.

"You are not in charge of this one, and we won't involve you."

Why the heck not? Why was he pushing me away when I was the one in the middle of all of this? "I can help. I know how he operates. I know how to find the girls. I have 1,500 women ready to help. Let's do a sting."

He chuckled. "No."

"What is your problem? It's not illegal to meet these women and offer them a way out. They come of their own will. Then I help them transition back to a normal life. The survivors will help me. We are so powerful. More powerful than you and your muscles and murder plans." I pointed into the room. The guys were talking quietly, but I couldn't hear a word.

Falcon looked to the ceiling and counted to three. When his eyes returned to mine, they were patient and unperturbed. "You need to let me handle this. If you interfere, I'll handcuff you to the bed and leave you there for days wearing nothing but a red ass and a ball gag."

I gulped and stared up into his bright blue gaze. With the bandage and bruises, he looked even more dangerous than before. I'd always thought of him as infallible, but his injuries made him human. We all bleed. We are all imperfect. I'd missed him so much and having him back felt good. Getting tied up sounded like fun, but I couldn't allow it.

He caught my look and his eyes heated. "You want that, I can arrange it for you." The corner of his sexy lips turned up and a warmth spread between my legs. Gah! This man!

"Take me to Gaspar now." I crossed my arms under my boobs and pouted.

"If Ivan is paying someone to hunt you down and kill you, eliminating Ivan gets rid of their money source. We save you first. We'll talk about a sting," he rolled his eyes, "later."

"Whatever. Take me to the hospital now."

He chuckled. "Alright."

"Fine." Something had changed with him. I couldn't put my finger on it, but he was making it challenging to stay angry at him.

"I'll be in my room." I spun on my heels and clicked away from him.

"GASPAR LOOKED SO WEAK. He's usually so strong. I hated seeing him like that."

We were back at the house after a full day at the hospital. I plopped on my bed and took off my heels. Falcon closed the door and sat in a chair next to a table in my room.

"I'd like to be alone," I said to him.

He shook his head. "Not leaving."

He'd been quiet all day, and I still had no clue where I stood with him. "You can go back to your strategy session with your commandos."

"Strategy can wait." His voice was tired. His eye looked less red and swollen, but he still needed to rest.

"I see no reason for you to remain in my room. If you wish to return to your job as bodyguard, you can stand outside the door."

"Like I said, not leaving."

"Why the hell not?"

"You need me."

Since when did he care what I needed? "I admit I'm shaken. It was very difficult seeing Diesel laid up in a hospital bed. And Gaspar is like my father. It would kill me to lose him. But I don't need you to comfort me. I need to be alone."

"We need to talk." He took a deep breath and leaned forward with his elbows on his knees.

Falcon kept getting weirder. He'd never asked me to talk about anything before. "About what?"

"About our arrangement."

Oh lord. "Our arrangement ended when you called me delusional and hoped I got my head blown off, which nearly happened, by the way, so thank you very much for wishing death on me."

"I fucked up." He leveled his sparkling blue eyes on me. I had to look away to resist the way they always made me want to drop my panties and spread my legs.

"Clearly. What else is new?"

He squeezed one eye shut and I watched my jab sink through him. Falcon and I knew all the right things to say to hurt each other.

"I want to fuck you."

Oh well, okay. He felt it too. "This is the deep talk we need to have?"

"I shouldn't have left."

No, he shouldn't have. "Okay. And?"

"I want us to keep fucking."

Too much had passed between us. We couldn't go backward. "Falcon, I'm not following you. Our arrangement for sex is over. I'm not interested anymore."

"I fucked up."

"Can you articulate a little better? Is this an apology? It's not working."

"I've never fucked the same woman more than twice."

"Never?"

"No. Only you."

"Are you saying I'm special?"

"I'm saying I want to see where this goes."

Oh. Wow. That was something. "So I'm supposed to feel honored to be the only woman you've fucked more than twice?"

"Yes."

"And you want to see where this goes?" Whatever the hell that meant.

"Yes."

My inner teenager jumped up out of her seat and clutched her hands over her chest. "By having more sex with me?"

He nodded.

Falcon was trying. He'd clearly never asked a girl to date him before. He was cute struggling with his words and it made me feel special to watch him squirm.

I decided to help him out. "Like a new arrangement?"

He nodded. "Let's call it an understanding."

This was my chance to get what I wanted. When men wanted sex, you could get them to agree to anything. "Before I agree to any understanding, I have one condition."

He raised his brow and wrinkled his forehead.

"You let me in on the mission to get Ivan."

"No."

"And we plan a sting. A big one. All the men you can find. My team helps too, and we rescue as many girls from Ivan as possible before you kill him."

He shook his head and looked out the window. "That's insane."

"Ivan ruining the lives of so many young girls is insane. It will take someone crazy to bring him down, and you are certifiably nutso. Those guys out there? Serious badasses, but I'd bet they have a streak of loco in them too. Tell them how many women Ivan has sold into trafficking, and they will be begging to be part of a sting."

"They know the numbers. We've faced this problem many times. They work in small cells. It's impossible to break down a large ring."

"We can do it. If you attack the top and I attack from the bottom, the middle will have nowhere to go."

His eyes looked over my face as I waited for his response. "Rogan has a buddy. Torrez. Ivan kidnapped his wife when she was a child. He forced her to marry his son. He abused her and kept her as a floor model for the other women he sold."

I sucked in a sharp breath. "Really?"

"Yeah."

"Oh my God. A lot of the girls had been kidnapped. I didn't know he went so far as to have them on display for sale."

"Torrez has a buddy, Zook. His wife, same thing."

"He needs to be stopped."

"Rogan had his step-father convince the U.N. to file an indictment. Waiting for him to leave the country."

"He might never leave the country."

"Torrez has a plan to infiltrate."

"Good. What's he planning?"

"Not sharing that with you."

"C'mon, Falc. Share or no understanding and no more sex." That would be sad, but this meant a lot to me. I'd do it if I had to.

"I don't want you involved." This time I saw true concern for my well-being in his eyes.

"I have the information you need to pull off something huge. Not just kill Ivan, but dismantle his infrastructure at the same time."

He leaned back and winced as he touched the bandage over his eye. "Alright. Let's negotiate. I'll let you in on plans for Ivan and any kind of sting operation we set up. But on the nights either of those events go down, you are handcuffed to the bed."

"Handcuffed? Do you mean literally or metaphorically?"

"You gonna stay out of any action?"

"Probably."

"Then it's metaphoric. Unless you'd like to be handcuffed to the bed while I'm out murdering someone. Does that turn you on?"

"Uh, no. I mean I'd be open to handcuffing me to the bed, but not if you leave, and definitely not while you're out risking your life."

He smirked. "Lots of information there. So you like handcuffs and you care about my life?"

"I didn't say that."

"You did."

"I said I'd probably agree to stay out of any action if I get to be part of the planning. Is that what you're offering?"

"Yes. You have good intel we can use. I gotta keep some things from you in case you're questioned."

"I can keep a secret. Ask the LASD and the FBI if they pulled anything out of me last night. They got nothing."

He stood and walked over to me. His eyes grew dark, and the heat from his fingers spread through my body as his hands gripped my hips.

He blinked twice before a white grin spread across his gorgeous face. "Ding, ding, ding. We have an understanding."

"No. We have one condition. I'm in on the planning of a sting."

"If a sting occurs."

"Right."

"I'd like to negotiate another condition." His eyes narrowed and his voice grew sinister. I was in way over my head with Falcon.

"What's that?" I swallowed the big lump in my throat.

"You get emotional, I fuck you."

A loud laugh burst from my lips. "No way."

"You bust out your diva act around me, I fuck you."

"No. Don't be ridiculous."

"You lie and manipulate me or anyone else, I fuck you."

"We are not having sex again. It's so not worth it. Hype. All hype."

He ignored my insult like I hadn't spoken. "You wear a dress that gives me and every man watching a hard-on..."

"You fuck me?"

"Ding, ding, ding. Another condition approved."

I laughed. He'd tricked me into that one. "I didn't agree."

"And our understanding starts right now. Did you have a rough day, honey?"

"You know I did."

"Feeling sad and worried?"

"Be quiet. It's not polite to joke about."

"Oh, I'm not joking. I am seriously going to fuck you right now."

His hands on my hips pulled me up against his hard body and, oh my God, very hard to say no to that but, "No."

His lips hit my neck and sucked. I allowed it for a second because it felt good. The sucking intensified and a sting sprouted in the spot.

I pulled back. "Don't give me a hickey."

"I thought you were off for a few weeks?"

"I am, but still. I can't be seen in public with a hickey!"

"Alright. I'll put it somewhere they can't see it."

"No, no." My forehead crashed to his chest.

He chuckled. "You need some time? Still upset about the shooting? I can give you that."

"Please. Let me go. I've had a horrible day. I need to rest and recover. I can't handle you right now and your tricks and games."

"Fine." He released me and stepped back. "No tricks. No games." He held his hands up in a peace offering. Oh my God, he was so cute.

"Thank you."

"But you will love our new understanding. Think about it. A long-term contract with the titanium dick." He grabbed his crotch and squeezed.

God, so vulgar. "Get out of here and go plan a murder."

He smiled and closed the door behind him.

Chapter 20

THAT NIGHT WE SLEPT in the same bed again without having sex. He'd worked all day and needed sleep to recover from his injuries. Thinking of Gaspar and Diesel in the hospital made my desire for him seem selfish and untimely. In the end, the distance he gave me made me feel respected and honored because he understood our situation, and he wanted to spend time with me even if he knew he wasn't getting sex.

Before I went down to look for Falcon the next morning, I put on a black skirt with a thin yellow stripe through the sheer ruffle at the knee. I paired it with a black and yellow bandeau blouse with off-the-shoulder sleeves. The gathered bodice clung to my ribs and tummy and ended in another ruffle at the hip.

I did my full makeup and hair routine, and added a red cardigan and matching sandals. I looked more put together than when I wore the robe, so hopefully my appearance would create less of a stir when I found Falcon and his friends.

No such luck.

They had the exact same reaction.

Going silent, looking up from their laptops, and staring at me with curious eyes. Two more men arrived last night, adding to the four who arrived yesterday. One bulky Latino with his hair shaved short and a gorgeous blue-eyed guy wearing a cowboy hat and a scruffy beard. He wasn't as big as the other guys and a little less intimidating, but also totally handsome. Did Falcon only play commando with hot guys?

Falcon stood up, a hint of a grin on his face and walked to me. Good to see he wasn't limping or clutching his side. "Hi," he said softly so that only I could hear.

"Hi," I answered back equally as soft. "Can I, uh, join you?"

My cheeks burned. Had a woman ever asked to join their secret justice league before? Did I want to join their group? The familiar nausea of stagefright roiled in my chest. Well, if I'd faced down rooms full of evil directors who would rip me to shreds, I could handle some hot-as-fuck commandos.

He frowned and his eyes settled on my lips. "No."

"We have an understanding, remember?" The details seemed fuzzy today, but I was pretty sure he'd agreed to let me sit in on strategy sessions. "C'mon. I'll sit quietly."

He stared at me as he deliberated. God, he could intimidate King Triton with his glare and the rugged strength of his jawline.

With a quiet grunt, he lowered his chin, placed his hand on the small of my back, and gave me a gentle push into the room.

Yay! I won.

We entered the room like the Beast escorting Belle into the ball. The six men stiffened and stared at Falcon like he'd just walked in with a kraken.

"This is Aida. She has intel on Ivan's operations at the street level. She finds the victims online and makes contact. She offers them assistance and helps them assimilate back into society."

Their eyes appraised me. I took a deep breath and gave them my audition smile. Confident yet humble.

"You know Rogan. This is Dallas, Ruger, Oz, Torrez, and Zook."

D, R, O, T, Z. I used my little trick to remember names when I first meet people. Got it.

"Can we trust her?" Dallas, the oldest of the bunch, asked. He had a few more wrinkles than the other guys and a hint of silver at his temples. Looked fabulous on him, by the way.

"Two days ago," Falcon responded, "After being shot at, she was interrogated by the LA Sheriff's Department and the FBI. She did not break and didn't let on a word about Ivan's connection to the bombing, the murders, or the shooting."

A few head nods and grunts of approval.

Good. I'd earned their respect.

I sat down next to Falcon and leaned back in my chair, crossing my legs at the ankles and my hands in my lap. My posture made it clear I intended to listen and not lead.

Rogan spoke first. "Torrez was briefing us on the Sharshinbaev's background."

I turned my gaze to Torrez and watched him throw a map toward the center of the table.

"Three palaces in Veranistaad. Zook and I got Soraya and Cecelia out of this one." He pointed to a map. Torrez kept his eyes down while he spoke but his voice scraped with a hard edge. "He's not a legitimate king. The monarchy died during the dissolution of the Soviet Union. He had three sons."

"Maksim is dead," Zook proclaimed in a deep, intimidating voice.

"Yegor's dead too," Torrez said with equal seriousness as he looked around the room.

Zook made eye contact with Torrez and something private passed between them.

"Killed by his brother," Torrez said casually. "The last remaining son, Pavel, fled the country. Hasn't been seen in months."

"Awesome." Zook grinned.

"Keep going," Rogan said, annoyed at whatever secret Zook and Torrez were sharing.

Torrez' eyes scanned the group of men. "NB Oil is a shell company. He ships weapons and women in cargo tankers. The network is nebulous. We've identified a few key handlers. He pays them to kidnap women and children and they receive a cut of any sale. He sells to anyone who will buy. Oil sheiks, Vegas pimps, Russian Bratva. He's known as the go-to man for trained virgins. Buyers pay top dollar for his girls."

Zook stood up and paced to the window.

"Rogan's mom and stepfather pushed for a United Nations indictment for murder, kidnapping, and human trafficking. The U.N. can't extradite Ivan. It's unclear what kind of diplomatic immunity he might have. The laws in his country are vague and rarely prosecuted. It's just a way of life there. The U.N. is our only hope for legal action, but we need to catch him leaving the country, and we need solid evidence. The word of two victims won't be enough."

"What are the odds of getting him by indictment?" Falcon asked.

"Based on the U.N.'s track record? Slim to none," Torrez responded.

"So we go after him," Falcon concluded.

Torrez and Falcon nodded at each other, both on the same page.

"I've been working on a plan," Torrez continued. "I set up a profile as a Saudi oil tycoon. I've been establishing a reputation as a buyer. Next step is to procure a meet with Ivan to discuss a big purchase. I go in alone, shoot him in the face, leave."

"Won't work. You won't get out alive," Rogan said. "We need him outside where we can snipe him from a rooftop."

"What if we turn some of the Russian tactics on them?" Falcon asked.

"Like what?" Rogan asked.

"We get the face-to-face and poison him. He dies of a heart attack. We walk out." Falcon spoke calm and confident.

"Could work," Torrez replied.

My mind drifted away from the details as Falcon's huge presence next to me became undeniable. He looked hot in his camo cargo pants and black tee. His goatee had grown thick and unruly. His hair was a little longer. It needed to come out of that tie so I could run my fingers through it and pull it.

Under the table, his hand slid over to my leg. The top of his palm pushed my skirt up, and his thick, warm fingers gave my knee a squeeze. Oh my God. My thighs clenched and my core turned hot. The intimacy of the simple gesture in the middle of a room of his peers had me struggling to keep a straight face.

"Dallas stays here to manage Aida's security detail." Rogan returning the conversation back to me captured my attention.

Dallas nodded at Rogan and glanced at me. His look said he'd keep me safe. I liked it.

"Blaze already told me he wants in," Rogan continued. "Torrez will take Diesel's place."

"So we all in?" Falcon asked.

Everyone grunted approval.

"Zook, you're out." Torrez spoke to Zook like he was used to giving him orders, but also a close friend.

"The hell I am."

"We can't risk you going back to prison."

"I did it before."

"Not with the same intentions we have this time. You watch over our women while we're gone"

Zook nodded. "Okay."

"Let's meet again tomorrow to assign tasks." Rogan stood and closed the laptop in front of him.

That was it? Meeting over? "Um, excuse me. What about the sting?"

Confused faces stared back at me.

"Aren't you planning the sting operation too?"

"I wasn't aware of any sting op." Torrez looked at Falcon.

"There is no sting op." He threw me a sideways warning glance.

"Well, there isn't yet. But we could make it happen," I said. "I think any attempt to take down Ivan needs to include something from the bottom up. You can take him out, but that won't help all the women he's already trafficked."

"What did you have in mind?" Rogan asked.

"A coordinated raid. Across every state. All at the same time. Find the women linked to him and offer them a way out."

"I already told you nothing we can do will make a dent in his system. It's too big." Falcon repeated his negative logic.

"Big systems fall apart the easiest." I repeated my argument.

"We don't have the financial resources or manpower for something of that scale," Falcon continued to shoot my idea down.

"Then we plan two or three stings. We just keep doing it until it makes a difference."

"That would require a full-time staff and resources." Rogan chimed in.

"Then let's hire a staff. Don't you have more guys on Team Sexy?"

"Team Sexy?" Ruger asked with a smile.

"You guys. Team Sexy."

They all chuckled and looked down.

Dallas tapped his pen like he was considering my proposal. "We have more guys. Not sure if any of them want to make a career talking prostitutes outta a job."

This was my chance to make a pitch for my girls. I stood up. "I don't know what kind of parents you have, but my mom was a whore." That got all their eyes on me. "My father probably a john. I grew up watching her under the thumb of a cartel leader named Manuel. One night when I was fifteen, Falcon came to the brothel. He got all the women out before his brother broke through the front door to kill us all. I was terrified. He was brave. He had a plan to get both me and my mother out, but Manuel took her minutes before Tivo, I mean Falcon, arrived."

They all looked at Falcon, surprised. Even Rogan. He hadn't told his closest friend? Falcon looked down, avoiding their gazes.

"So Falcon took me alone and helped me start a new life in New Jersey. My mother loved opera. She never got to see one because he forced her to sleep with twenty men a night. Never a day off. And if she didn't make her quota, he beat her till she bled. I nursed her wounds. I watched my mother go through that. She'd be bruised and battered and insist on going back to work because she feared what Manuel would do to me. Can you imagine a life like that? I wonder all the time how horrible it must have been for her. We never found her. I've searched everywhere, but just think of the life she could've had if she had left with Falcon and me that night. She could go to the opera and watch me sing. She could marry and have a man love her. Those women, they are all my mother. You see? They all deserve a chance at happiness, and no one has the right to take that from them. So, yeah, we need to find the resources and the funding because it's important. Someone has to do it, and I know how and so do you. It's our obligation as human beings to fight against this. You see? Do you see what I mean?" Tears stung behind my lids. The men stared silently at me, expecting me to say more. But I didn't have any more. I had nothing.

Falcon stood, wrapped an arm around me, and tucked my side into his chest.

"I'll fund it." One voice from Team Sexy broke the heavy silence. I turned to see the sound came from Torrez. "I'll fund it. You want one sting? I'll fund it. You want a permanent operation, I'll fund it."

"I'll provide the manpower," Dallas said.

Oh my gosh. They heard me. They said yes! "Thank you. Thank you so much."

"I'm not sure what she's doing isn't against the law." Rogan spoke up.

Dallas looked at him. "Don't care."

"Don't care either." Torrez mimicked Dallas's response.

I tried to suppress my joy, but I couldn't stop the huge smile that grew on my lips. Team Sexy got even sexier when they smiled back at me.

"Alright. That's enough," Falcon said, his voice irritated.

"What?" I looked up at him. This was good news.

"We gotta go." He grabbed my arm and hauled me out of the room. I managed to get in a quick wave and a goodbye to the men at the table, but they were all grinning and looking down.

Darn Falcon. I was earning their respect and getting what I wanted, and he went all caveman on me.

He ducked into the first door in the hallway, which happened to be the laundry room, and pressed me up against the closed door.

The pressure when his body hit mine knocked a gust of breath out of me. "What?"

"You broke the conditions of our understanding."

"I never agreed to anything." Did I?

"You pulled a diva move, you manipulated them, got emotional, and you made us all hard."

I laughed and spat back, "I did not!"

"So I get to fuck you four times." His lips crashed down on mine, his scruff scratching the sensitive skin around my lips.

The people in my life always treated me like fragile porcelain but Falcon didn't care. He attacked me however he wanted. Opera singer or not, he took me rough every time.

His hand gripped behind my knee and my skirt stretched tight as he hitched my leg over his hip. His hips pushed the skirt the rest of the way up, and he ground his hard cock into my abdomen.

Oh my lord in heaven, it was divine.

His lips released mine and skimmed down my throat to the top of my cleavage. "Fuck this top." He growled and his free hand yanked the top down in the center, revealing my black strapless bra. He kissed the newly-revealed skin of my breasts.

I tugged on his ponytail to try to stop him, but Falcon buried his nose between my breasts and reached back under my shirt to unsnap the bra.

"Your friends are in the next room."

My bra fell loose and he tugged it away as he stretched the fabric of my shirt and tucked it under my breasts, offering them up to him like a buffet. He bit down hard on one nipple and teased it with his tongue.

"Oh my God." My hands gripped his neck as my head thunked on the door.

He stopped and kissed my lips again, letting his thumb rub the moisture from his mouth into my nipple. With his lips against mine he said, "Moan for me."

"No. They'll hear."

He grinned. He loved the challenge. Then the ground left my feet, the room spun, and I found my ass on top of a cold hard washing machine. He reached behind me, and my butt started to rumble.

Okay so dryer, not washing machine. A dryer he turned on which hummed and buzzed underneath me.

"Lie back." He pushed my shoulders until I was forced to support myself by my elbows, my naked breasts totally available to him. I could only reach him with my legs, so I pulled him close, and his mouth latched onto my nipple again.

A grunt escaped from deep in my throat. "God, Falcon."

I was able to work one hand around his neck and pull his hair tie out. His gorgeous long brown hair fell forward over his face and caressed my breasts.

His head moved down my stomach, his hair trailing behind. How could one man be so sexy? Impossible.

He yanked my skirt up higher, ripped my panties off, and forced my legs wide open. My head lolled back.

He dove into my pussy and kissed my clit with the same passionate tongue he used to kiss my lips. I bit my lip to stifle the moan. He looked up at me. "Let it out. They can't hear."

"Falcon, my voice projects across a crowded amphitheatre. They will certainly hear me in the next room even with the dryer going."

"They'll think we're having a lot of fun doing laundry. C'mon." He forced his fingers inside me and rubbed my G-spot at the same time his tongue tortured my clit. The dryer started to heat up my ass. The rumbling of the dryer made everything heightened. "C'mon."

And with that I let go. I couldn't hold it back anymore a long low moan emerged from deep in my throat and filled the small laundry space. They had to have heard it in the living room.

He kept at me till I pulled his hair.

His head came up and he kissed me. "Fucking fantastic."

Then the room spun again, and I found myself with my front pressed up against the running dryer. He positioned me so my hips hit the edge and the rumbling permeated my core. "Oh."

"Feel good?" I braced my hands on the cupboard above the dryer and listened to him unleash the beast. The cool titanium ball of his apa touched my ass. He teased it up and down between my cheeks, leaving a small trail of pre-come behind.

He reached up and the dryer went into overdrive. The rumbling tripled, the vibrations rocked my core, and his hand on my back pushed me down for maximum contact with the metal machine.

I groaned.

"Stay like that. Right there."

"Yes."

His cock found my entrance and he teased it with the tip. So big and so hard.

"Wet and hot for me." He kept running the tip through the moisture there, teasing me. "You on the pill?"

What? He wanted to do this without a condom? "Yes," I gasped out.

His hand between my shoulder blades pushed my torso down until my nipples hit the top of the machine. Hot vibrations ripped from my nipples to my core. Holy shit. He had me buzzing everywhere.

"Ready?"

"Yes." I could barely speak.

Slowly, he worked the tip inside me from behind. My opening resisted the balls of the apa, creating delicious tension that must have hurt him. He groaned as the tension broke. The other piercings slid inside with small pops as he filled me.

"Your hot wet tight pussy loves my cock."

I couldn't respond but I didn't need to. It was obvious he spoke the truth. He bottomed out and I felt full. Full of all the glory that went with Falcon. His size, his strength, his intensity, all of it filled me up till I couldn't take it anymore.

He lost control and began to ram me into the machine. Each thrust forced me deeper into the vibrations. I wiggled my hips to get the feeling right on my clit.

"Oh God, there."

"Yes, baby. Stay like that. Stay like that, and I'll make you feel good."

He rammed into me, building speed and strength until I thought we would both explode. The most glorious pressure pushed through me. I gasped for breath as I came hard. He was relentless, not breaking stride for a second to allow me to recover.

My nipples tingled, his cock hit my G-spot, and the machine made naughty vibrations on my clit.

He forced another orgasm out of me and I moaned. Loud.

His breath hitched, he planted himself deep and groaned in my ear. We came together like we were both in a canoe toppling over the falls.

God, it felt so good. The greatest high, the deepest love. We became one in our shared euphoria.

Eventually he slowed, and his arm slipped under me to support my weight. "Phenomenal, mi paloma. You are so damn beautiful. Blows my fucking mind every time." His breath tickled my ear as he cradled me from behind. I loved these moments with Falcon when the storm had passed, and his voice became soft and affectionate.

My fifteen-year-old self swooned in his arms. *He's a superhero.*

No, no, no. No swooning. No giving in to the warm afterglow of sex with Falcon. Shoot. I shouldn't have even given in to the sex. He'd hurt me, and I hadn't forgiven him. I couldn't trust him at all.

"I'm ready to go again but want you up in the bed." He pulled out and turned me in his arms. He found a folded towel above the washer and wiped between my legs.

His touch seemed sweet, gentle, loving. He lowered my skirt and rose to plant another kiss on my lips.

"We should get to the hospital to see Gaspar and Diesel," I said between kisses. He couldn't really mean to hold me to his conditions? Four times in a row?

He shook his head and bit his lower lip with his teeth. "Unh-uh. Three more. You're gonna be worn out as hell when you walk into that hospital. They might have to admit you for pussy fatigue."

I slapped his chest and he laughed. "Stop it."

"Ready?"

"I can't go out there. It's too humiliating. I know they heard me."

"First of all, they are not the type to eavesdrop. In the military, you overhear a lot of things and learn to tune out to give a brother privacy. Second, they all absolutely adore you and whatever respect they had for you before is off the charts now they know you light up for me and let it go. No shame in that. None at all."

He nabbed my panties off the floor and tucked them in his pocket. He guided me out of the laundry room with a casual hand on my back. Like two people walking out of the laundry room made complete sense. We had a housekeeper do the laundry. Thank God she wasn't here this morning.

Falcon walked me up to our bedroom with confidence in his step. He didn't seem to have any doubts we could go three more rounds, but my hands were shaking with nerves.

In my room, I looked up into his heated blue eyes. So pretty and mesmerizing.

Lord help me.

We did it three more times, and I was totally worn out. Falcon called Blaze to tell him we'd be late for our visit.

AFTER WE'D DOZED FOR a bit, I summoned the courage to ask him a question. "How long will it last?"

His body was curled behind me, one of his legs pushing mine forward in a half-spooning position. "What last?"

"Our hypothetical new understanding. If I agree, which I haven't yet, how long would we keep this up?"

His soft breath tickled the sensitive hairs at the base of my scalp. "Indefinitely," he said low and sleepy.

Oh no. He would not play with my heart as long as he liked and then leave. When my body tensed, his hand came up and smoothed my hair away from my face gently.

"Espera y verás, mi paloma."

Wait and see, my dove.

I would have fought him if I wasn't completely relaxed and lost in a multi-orgasm cloud and I didn't love that idea.

"Okay."

Chapter 21

———

THORNE AND I SAT SIDE-by-side next to Gaspar's bed-side. We'd sent Marcella home to get some much needed rest as we waited for Gaspar to wake up.

Thorne curled his fingers and inspected his nails. "So what's the status between you and the Egyptian warrior with the enormous pierced cock?"

"Thorne, my goodness." I glanced at Gaspar to make sure he hadn't moved. "He might be unconscious, but he can proba-bly hear us."

Thorne stopped mid-action from bringing his fingers to his mouth and abruptly forced his hands flat on his lap. "Gaspar, if he were awake, would ask you the same thing. He adores you like I do."

I patted the top of Gaspar's hand. It felt cold and lifeless. "Please, Papá. Don't listen to Thorne. Just come back to us."

Thorne leveled a disapproving gaze at me and bit into his fingernail, making that cutting sound I hated so much. "You didn't answer my question. How is the bird of prey?"

"He is... infuriating the fuck out of me." I squeezed Gaspar's hand. "Forgive my language, Papá, but if you woke up and I told you what Falcon is doing, you'd let out a few choice words too."

"What's he doing?" Thorne frowned and forced his hands to clasp in his lap.

"He's pestering me."

"For sex?" he whispered.

"Yes. No. I don't know."

"What does he want?"

"He wants to *wait and see*."

"Ooh, yay!" He sat up and smiled.

"Not yay. What the hell does that even mean?"

"It means he wants to wait and see where it goes." His hand flew up to his mouth again. He really needed to get that under control.

"Oh please. Don't give me that line. He tried that. I know where it will go. He'll use me up and discard me like all the others."

"It might go that way. But wouldn't it be wonderful if it went another way?"

"I doubt that will happen." I stared at his finger in his mouth and tilted my head to remind him to stop.

He pulled his hand away and looked at it like it had a mind of its own. Shame passed through his eyes, frustrated with himself again for letting his nail-biting compulsion get out of control. "I've known for a long time you guys would never keep it casual. You are a sweet soul, and you don't have that callousness in you."

"Hush. That is not true. I'm a mean sonofabitch."

He laughed. "You play the role, but you are as weak as a newborn fawn."

"Be quiet."

"He needs it."

"Well let him find some other married woman, not me."

"I think he needs *you*."

I didn't respond.

"Have you looked in his eyes?"

"Who hasn't? They're hypnotic."

"Mmm-hmm. Absolutely true. If he liked men, I'd never let him fuck me from behind. Always on my back so I could look in his eyes while he came."

"Uh, Thorne. Please. Don't get carried away."

He turned his whole body toward me, his hand gripping the chair as if to keep it from his mouth. "Oh, right. Right. Okay. So his eyes. Really look at them. Not when you're fucking because who could concentrate? I mean most of the time. When you look at his eyes. What do you see?"

"Nothing. He's closed."

"Exactly. He's rusted. Like Gaspar says..."

"If you don't use it, you rust," I completed his thought.

He nodded. "He hasn't used it in a while. Whatever he's been through. Maybe serving in the military, maybe his bodyguard work, or his family... It's rusted his heart. Something about you greases his joints. Has he told you anything?"

"Not much. It's complicated. There's so much you don't know." I shook my head, so much nobody knew.

"Oh tell, tell."

"We have history," I said, resigned, hoping he'd stop asking questions.

"You do?" No, of course he wouldn't stop.

I wanted to talk about it, but keep it vague. "If it weren't for Falcon, my life would've been very different."

His eyebrows flew up. "He changed your life? How?"

Sharing this with Thorne meant facing a lot of truths I'd long avoided, but maybe it was time. "I never told you the details. The night I lost my mother, Falcon rescued me. He saved the lives of a lot of women, but he took me to New Jersey. He introduced me to Soledad. He told her to take me to New York and put me in art school. He paid for it."

"He... Yes, you told me about a man who saved your life and was out there looking for your mom. The superhero?"

"Yeah." I hadn't told anyone else about him. I trusted Thorne. I was never sure if Thorne believed my superhero was real. I always assumed he thought I made it up to comfort myself.

"That's him? He's your superhero?"

"Yeah."

He bit his lip and his eyes glistened. "But he didn't find her?" he whispered.

"No." I looked away as I whispered back.

"Oh sweetie." He took my hands in his and the rough skin of his abused fingers brushed my palm. "I'm so sorry. You've been going through all this without sharing?"

"I haven't faced it. I pushed it down deep." I squeezed his hands.

"Yes, you try to do that, but the truth always surfaces and we have to deal with the fall out."

"Yes."

"So let's face it. You feel grateful to him?"

I nodded. Fifteen-year-old Magdalena nodded too. Both of us with tears welling in the corners of our eyes.

"But you're also angry he didn't find her?"

I closed my eyes and two tears dropped. "Yes." I was angry at him for not keeping his promise, but I also understood how difficult it would be to find my mother. She could have been anywhere in the world. She could've been dead.

He leaned over in his chair and embraced me. "This is amazing."

I sniffled.

"Do you know why he's rusted?" he asked me.

"No." I had no idea.

"You need to find out."

"I don't know if he'll tell me. Maybe I don't want to know. He has a dark soul."

"Don't we all?"

I laughed. "I guess so."

"So wait and see." He smirked.

I gave him a doubtful look.

"Be the steel wool to scrub away his rust."

"Thorne..." I tried to stop him, but he was on a roll.

"If the steel wool doesn't work, try vinegar."

I laughed.

"Baking soda. Try hydrogen peroxide. Try a blowtorch! But get him unrusted!"

"You are so funny." We laughed for a bit before sitting quiet for a while watching Gaspar sleep. Thorne's hand came up to his mouth, but I stopped him from taking a bite. "I will hold your hand so you don't bite your fingers."

He looked up at me with one of his big brown eyes. "Thank you, but I want a divorce." His brows went up like he was surprised the words came out of his mouth.

"What?"

"I want you to divorce me," he said more firmly.

"Thorne, our arrangement..."

"Has served its purpose."

"C'mon. If this is about Falcon..."

"Two years is an eternity in Hollywoodland. No one thinks you're a vampire. My brother is eighteen and out of the house. It's time for me to face my parents."

We weren't a couple, but losing him would hurt like losing a boyfriend. "I don't want to divorce you. You're my best friend."

He patted my hand. "As your best friend, I'm divorcing you. I'll have a lawyer draw up the papers. It's done."

This was unfair. "I'm sad. I don't approve."

"Nature abhors a vacuum, my love. Into my role, a new man will appear."

"Who?"

"Wait and see." His eyes sparkled and he hugged me again. He felt skinny. I should take him to lunch after this, someplace fattening.

"I need Gaspar back, and then I'll be able to face Falcon and a divorce."

His hands squeezed my upper arms, forcing me to sit up straight. "What if Gaspar doesn't come back to us?"

My gaze turned to Gaspar in the bed. His normally vibrant face pale, his warm skin looking white and cold. Is that what he would look like when he died? "Don't say that. Please. I don't know what I'd do without him. How could I sing? How could I love? Life would not be worth living."

He shook my shoulders to draw my attention back to him. "No. If we lose him, we'll mourn, we'll say goodbye, and we'll carry on. That's how life is. We carry on."

Gaspar coughed and we both looked at him, waiting. A barely there noise came from his chest. Then a hum. Only three notes, but I recognized them as the first three notes of a song he'd written with John Denver, "Perhaps Love."

"Oh my God. Oh my God. Call the nurse! He's waking up!" Thorne's voice hit the ceiling, it was so high-pitched.

We both skittered around the room with our hands up. Neither one of us knew how to call the nurse! She just came in on schedule. We hadn't needed to call her!

Falcon poked his head in and back out. Thorne and I were still wandering around the room when the nurse came in and saw to Gaspar.

I held Thorne's hand as she asked Gaspar questions, and he mumbled some answers and coughed.

Thorne and I cried as we stood there smiling beside the bed. Marcella rushed in and broke into tears when she saw him awake. She fell over his chest. His hand came up and clasped her head. He hummed a few more notes of "Perhaps Love."

Falcon came in and looked at me. Our gazes locked. A slow grin spread across his face, and his eyes lit up as he opened his arms. I let go of Thorne's hand and ran to Falcon. The heat and strength of his chest and arms pulled me in and held me close. "He's awake," I said to his pecs. "He's back."

"That's good."

"Do you think he'll be okay?"

"We'll have to wait and see."

Chapter 22

———

BACK AT THE HOUSE, Falcon poured Godiva chocolates into a bowl on the coffee table.

"Do you like chocolate?" I asked him.

"No but you do."

"How did you know that?"

"Found them in your closet." He sat down on the couch and stretched out.

He'd been poking around in my closet? What else did he find? "And you decided to set them out on the coffee table?"

Leaning back, his eyes serious, he leveled his gaze on me. "If you like them, you should eat them. Don't hide them in your closet like contraband. Eat. Enjoy. No shame."

Nice idea, but the media placed a lot of pressure on me to watch my figure. "I'll lose track and eat them all."

"Then eat them all," he said, like it was simple.

"I can't."

"Then I'll count them for you."

I sat down next to him, and he wrapped an arm around my neck. "Here's number one." He handed me a purple truffle.

I smiled and opened the wrapper. "How many do I get to eat?"

"How many do you want to eat?"

"I want to eat the whole bowl. But should probably stick to two or three a day."

He nodded, but didn't take a chocolate for himself. "You happy?" he asked me.

I had just plopped the truffle in my mouth, so of course I was very happy. I held up my finger while I enjoyed it. His eyes grew dark as he watched me chew. I finished it and licked my lips.

"Jesus, woman. Your daily limit just went up to ten."

"I can't eat ten a day."

"Twenty."

I laughed, and his eyes sparkled with his grin. "You look happy."

"I am. Gaspar will sing and conduct again. It's such a relief."

"Good."

He lifted my hips and pulled me around to straddle him.

"Uh, is anyone here?"

"Nope. Now we can talk."

For a man who never talked, he'd been keen to talk the last few days. "About what?"

"You ever shot a handgun?"

Oh, well. Not what I expected. "No." Obviously not.

"You're going to today. I'm gonna teach you."

Uh oh. "I don't need..."

"From what I can see, you have no plans of abandoning your vigilante hooker rescue business. If something goes wrong, I want you to be prepared."

"I really don't want to do that." Falcon was pushing my limits again, forcing me to face stuff I worked hard to stuff down.

"Why?"

I hated to admit it to him, but he was asking me honestly so I owed him the truth. "Guns terrify me."

His hands tightened on my legs and his brow scrunched. "I always have weapons on me. Didn't notice you feeling un-comfortable."

"I hide it well."

He nodded. "Is this new since Ivan's been after you? Some se-rious shit has gone down."

"It's been worse lately, but honestly? It started one night in a brothel when Oscar de la Cruz busted in shooting wildly."

"Ahh, I see." He looked down, probably remembering the night he killed his brother, and possibly feeling guilty for my fear of guns today. Whatever he thought, he processed it internally before he looked up at me. "So your response is to deny you're scared?"

"Yes."

"The way to fight anxiety is to face it. Gain confidence you will know what to do in an emergency."

I shook my head. "I don't think I could ever shoot anyone."

"It gets easier with practice. Let's go." He patted my thigh.

"No seriously. I'm really scared. I can't do that."

"I'll show you. Been around guns since I was in diapers. And I'm still alive. You gotta get over shooter anxiety, or you'll spend your life in fear."

Panic itched its way up my throat.

The girls on the dock. Gaspar getting shot. No guns. No.

"There is no one better to teach you how to shoot a handgun than me. C'mon."

He grabbed my hand and walked us into the laundry room. I shivered remembering the intimate time we'd spent on the dryer. He slid a key card under a shelf on the wall. It dropped open revealing several handguns and boxes of ammo inside.

"This one's my favorite." He held up a gun and grinned at it. He looked back to me. "You need something more compact." He picked up a gun that looked exactly the same as the other gun.

My mouth went dry and goosebumps peppered my arms.

He swiped a box of bullets, closed his secret shelf, and walked out. "Let's go."

"Falcon. I'm feeling very nervous about this." Like about to barf nervous.

"Respect for weapons is always good."

Oh lord. He was not giving up.

I tried another approach. "If I have you, I don't need to know how to shoot."

"I can't be everywhere. Chaos reigns in a battle situation. You need to be prepared."

"Battle?" My voice squeaked.

"Ivan sent men to blow up a concert, shot six women dead, and shot Gaspar and Diesel. It's not a battle, it's a war."

"Oh. Won't the neighbors freak out?"

"The property is huge. With the big canyon out back, we'll be fine."

My hands shook as I followed him to the back yard.

He set the stuff he'd gathered on the patio table.

"First rule. Never point it at anyone you don't want dead."

I nodded but I felt like crying. I didn't want to shoot a gun.

"Load the magazine here." He pushed the ammo up into the handle of the gun. "Rack the slide." He slid the top part back like I'd seen done in movies. "You see a bullet?" He showed me the top of the gun.

"Yes." I saw what looked like a bullet inside a tube.

"It's loaded, a cartridge in the chamber." He stepped away from me, spread his legs, and aimed the gun toward the canyon behind the house.

"One foot back, fighting stance. Take aim and..."

The loud pop hit my ears. I didn't even see the bullet, but a faint thud in the brush meant the bullet hit something. A casing had popped out the side and clinked on the slate patio. He lowered the gun and smiled at me. "Got it?"

He looked incredibly hot and comfortable, but no, I didn't get any of it.

"Try it."

"No, really. I'm scared." My stomach flipped. I could not do this.

"I'll help you." He moved behind me and lifted my arms. He placed the gun in my right hand but didn't give me its weight. As he arranged my hands, he spoke softly in my ear. "Proper grip gets rid of recoil. You control your recoil, you have the upper hand."

I was listening, but the fear combined with his closeness made it hard to concentrate.

"Think of it as an extension of your body. Not a thing you're holding, but your actual arm and hand."

He adjusted my palm higher. "Place your shooting hand high up on the beavertail, gives you the mechanical advantage, but never above it because you don't want to get hit by the slide. Thumbs forward. Angle your left hand and place it butt-up against your right. No space between for the push back to get through. Solid." He pulled my arms in front of us, his big arms cradling mine. "Make sure your arm is straight in line with the barrel. That energy is gonna come back at you, and you need to be ready. Aim for that tree trunk."

His right foot wrapped around my shin and pushed my foot back. This made me fall deeper into him, and I felt his hard body all along my back.

"Let your finger fall naturally on the trigger."

"Nothing feels natural."

"Try it. Where would you put your finger?"

I slipped my index finger on the cold metal trigger.

"There. That's your sweet spot."

His hands tightened over mine. "Keep your grip hard. Strong and even on both sides. Like a vise. You're in control of that weapon. You're going to make it do what you want it to do, and mistakes aren't going to happen because you are confident and unyielding."

"I'm not feeling confident at all."

"Fake it. You're an actress. Put on your best Charlie's Angels' face and make me believe it."

This made sense. Yes. When he put it that way, I could tackle the fear. I tucked my chin and furrowed my forehead, giving the imaginary audience my badass face of fury.

"Good. Before you shoot, make sure you know the person is a direct threat. Never shoot someone unarmed or on your own team."

"Can't I just run?"

"Sometimes you can't run. You have to stand and fight."

"Okay."

"Brace your arms, pull the trigger back slow, and hold it down after the shot."

"Now?"

"Yes. Send it."

"Oh God. Okay." My arms felt weak and my hands shook, but Falcon's steady presence all around me helped quell the panic. I held my breath and pulled. The blast burst from my hands, and the gun jumped back. Falcon's hands tightened and supported mine. I gasped and a nervous laugh escaped my throat. I glanced down at the ground.

"Don't react to the recoil and spent cartridge. Focus on the next shot. Let the trigger up till you feel the click."

I did what he said and felt the click.

"Keep your eye on the front sight. Pull your next shot."

I followed his directions with his arms supporting me. The second blast felt just as loud and scary. "I did it!"

"Yes." His voice sounded like he was proud of me. "Now by yourself."

He slowly removed his arms, but I felt his front close to my back. My heart pounded in my chest.

"Send another."

My brain scrambled to remember all he'd said. Straight arms, hard grip, look at the sight, pull the trigger.

The next shot exploded out of the gun. This time, I saw a trace of the bullet sailing off into the canyon.

"I did it!" I didn't think I'd hit the tree, but I'd shot the gun!

"No celebrating. If you're in an emergency situation, empty your magazine. You'll probably miss and you only get one chance. If you've determined you need to kill that person, unleash all you got. Now send another."

I shot four more rounds by myself. Each time became easier, and I thought one hit the tree.

"Excellent. One last thing."

"Yes?"

He wrapped his arms around me again and took the gun between both our hands, keeping it pointed at the ground. His lips came down and his deep voice rumbled in my ear. "Make your first magazine count. Assume you won't have time to reload."

"This is so scary."

"I'll do all that I can to make sure you never have to fire a handgun. And if you do, I promise I'll be there before you need to reload. Ask Rogan. He knows I always cover him."

"Wow. That sounds like a nice friendship."

"Your life is in their hands, you're more than friends. You're brothers."

I nodded and a warm breeze from the canyon blew over us. He closed his shoulders around me, his hands, and the gun inching toward me. "Um."

"You feel more comfortable now?" Something warm touched my abdomen. I looked down to see his hand pressing the gun flat on my stomach. His other hand massaged my hip. My toes tingled, and the hair on the back of my neck danced.

"Yes," I breathed. It was not nearly as terrifying as I thought it would be. I had faced my fear and succeeded and with him behind me, it was thrilling. I could see why Falcon was attracted to the power and skill required to shoot a gun accurately.

"You see how the gun is part of me?" His hand with the gun inched up my stomach, stopping under my breasts.

"I see how incredibly sexy you are when you handle one. You're a good teacher too. I enjoyed my lesson."

"Watching you give it a try is arousing." His other hand grabbed my thigh and squeezed as he sunk his teeth into my neck and started sucking.

I tilted my head and closed my eyes. The man's hot mouth always reduced me to mush. "You find my fear stimulating?"

He stood so close, the potent energy ricocheted in the space between us. "Mmm. Everything about you stimulates me."

God, his raspy voice sent a jolt straight to my nipples. His hand with the gun trailed up my chest. I bit my lip and held my breath as the barrel brushed my nipple.

"Uh, are there bullets in there?"

"No." He lifted the gun, pulled the slide back and showed me the empty chamber. He popped out the magazine and placed it on the table. "Not loaded. Just playing."

Oh my, not loaded. Did that make this any less lethal?

He ran the barrel back and forth across my nipple. His hand spanned my stomach and tugged me back against him, smashing his hard cock into the crease of my ass.

"Falcon..."

I gasped as his foot kicked the inside of mine out and his knee bent in, molding our bodies together as one. "You wet for me?"

I closed my eyes and groaned, struggling to absorb all the majesty Falcon was giving me.

"Dangerous metal caressing your skin. Bet you're soaked."

He knew me too well. I was wet between my legs before the lesson ended and totally turned on now. He trailed his teeth up my neck and jaw to my mouth. As I lost myself in the kiss, he slipped the tip of the gun inside my blouse, worked it under my bra, and swiped it over my nipple. His hand around my hips moved down and cupped between my legs. My body lit up for him. With the California sun setting on us, the picturesque canyon beyond the house, and his talented tongue working magic in my mouth, I felt entranced. I reached up and tugged his hair to deepen the kiss. He was a necromancer and I'd fallen under his spell.

After awhile, he groaned and gently removed the gun from my bra. He turned me to face him. Once he had full access, his tongue dove in deep, challenging me to fight back. We both grunted and pulled each other closer. We had to answer this urgent call and it couldn't wait.

Something hard pressed between my legs. Oh shit. The gun. I broke the kiss. "Falcon..." How far would he take this?

"It's part of me. Don't you want it inside you?"

What? "You're not putting that thing inside me."

He pressed his lips to mine and grinned. "No?"

"No."

He slid the barrel of the gun over my sex and I gasped.

"What if I keep it on the outside?"

Oh my God, was he asking permission to get me off with a gun? He bent down and reached for the hem of my skirt. He raised it slowly, exposing my thighs and ass to any of the neighbors with binoculars. Not to mention, his crew of commandos could return to the house at any moment.

"Just right here." His voice pleaded as he massaged the gun over my underwear. He wanted it bad. It meant something to him I would probably never understand. Maybe he wanted me to face my fear of guns, or maybe he wanted me to accept that guns were a huge part of his life. The man needed to learn to express himself with words, because this form of communication was hazardous to my health.

The tip of the gun dialed in on my clit. He kissed me, forcing my back to arch while his firm arm supported the small of my back. His mouth crashed down on my lips and he kissed me with the same rhythm as his strokes. The gun became sandwiched between us as he moved his hips closer to mine, but he maintained total control, not missing one beat or giving me any breaks. He didn't hesitate or back off.

"Let me put it inside you," he said against my lips.

Oh my lord, he wanted to take it further. "I don't know."

"Let go and try something new. You're safe and you want it bad."

It was crazy and reckless. I had no idea why I wanted it, but I did and he sensed it coming off me. "Okay," I whispered.

His mouth turned up in a grin like I'd given him a present. Falcon wasn't the kind of man you could buy a material gift for. He fed off this kind of test of trust and limit pushing. He kissed down my chest and fell to his knees where his head was at a level he could see everything.

He used his gun like a hand, moving my panties aside and gliding down to tease my sensitive parts with the metal. I balanced my weight on his shoulders, and my body locked up.

"Relax, mi paloma. I got you in my hands right here."

I moaned and clawed at his shoulders as my body became weak and I surrendered. Only with Falcon could I let go like this and indulge in something new and scary. I'd never let anyone else touch me with a gun, but his fearlessness broke down all my defenses. No more diva or fame, no bodyguard, no threats. Only him and I existed as we trusted each other with something we both wanted.

"Yeah, baby. Yeah." He kept up his relentless teasing on my clit with his weapon as his raw, unguarded eyes watched with intense fascination. This made him come alive like it was some long-held secret fantasy of his. He was sharing part of himself with me and God, it was resplendent.

I gasped as I felt the gun work deeper between my legs and become slick with my wetness. He stared in locked concentration, watching the gun we had just fired sink inside me. "Fuck, yeah." His voice was a low rasp. The thick metal stretched me until his fingers reached my opening. His mouth latched onto my clit, and he worked the gun out and back in. He hummed and I knew he loved this. It felt phenomenal.

My nails dug into his neck as I felt my orgasm rise in me. He moved my leg up over his shoulder to get better access. I threw my head back and moaned as I fell over the edge. A wave of pleasure shot through me like a bullet. He continued to work the gun in and out as the involuntary pulses clenched around the barrel, moving on his fingers pressed there. We'd made a deadly mess and he had a front row seat to view it.

As I caught my breath, he carefully withdrew the gun and helped me stand up straight. He wrapped his arms behind me and grinned.

I smiled back at him.

"You just rocked my world." His grin grew in a luxurious smile.

"Mine feels tilted on its axis."

The gun slid out from between us, and his hard dick pressed against me through his pants. "Let's go upstairs."

"No, let's stay here," I replied. Upstairs felt much to far away.

He glanced around the yard and his eyes stopped at the side of the house that led to the front door. "Upstairs, baby."

Uh oh. Did someone see us?

I nodded, pulled my skirt down and walked in front of him into the house. The slippery wetness between my legs rubbed my skin as he followed me silently up the stairs. The second we hit my room, he closed the door, set the gun down, and moved on me lightning fast.

He tugged off my clothes and our arms tangled as I worked open his pants. He groaned and forced my back to the bed as he lifted my leg behind the knee and pierced me with his hard cock.

"Yes, God, yes." It felt so good, his rigid dick moving in and out of me. The sexy roll of his hips, the dark hairs on his abdomen undulating with his thrusts. Falcon's intense eyes on me, dark with desire and lust.

He'd worked up a sweat, and we mashed together in a hot, wet, sticky mass. His lids lowered, and he powered home. I closed my eyes and let the glory of it all roll through me. He grunted to get my attention. Yes, we needed to look at each other through this. I needed to see what I did to him and he wanted to show me.

His thrusts sped up and I could feel it growing like a river up against a dam. Higher, deeper until the dam broke and the pressure gushed out. I moaned a loud, drawn out cry and throbbed around his dick, panting and gasping for breath. His chin came up, exposing his gorgeous Adam's apple.

Falcon groaning out his climax while coming inside me had to be the most carnal act I'd ever seen. I was lucky to witness something so rare. I'd made the right decision by saying yes and allowing us to share this moment.

He collapsed on me and kissed me hard. He stopped, rested his head on my chest, and proceeded to let out a long chain of curse words in Spanish. It was some long sentence about how he died a thousand deaths and came back to life in my sweet pusssy.

I caressed his head and laughed.

It was beautiful.

Chapter 23

AN HOUR LATER, FALCON still held me in his arms. The sun had set and he hadn't constructed his chilly wall between us like he always did when he left the bed immediately following sex.

I offered up a silent plea.

Stay. This time, stay.

Maybe fucking me with a gun was what he needed to lower his guard. Trusting him with my life was a huge leap of faith for me. Hopefully, he understood and appreciated the gesture. Far more meaningful than physical gratification, we connected on the deepest level possible.

Slowly, almost reluctantly, he disengaged our limbs and slid out of bed. I watched him pull on his pants and sit in a chair on the opposite side of the room.

He didn't turn on the lights, but in the evening shadows, I saw his body slumped and a forlorn grimace on his face. I'd lost him again to his demons.

"Come back to bed."

"Gotta clean my gun." His voice scratched.

He stood up and took his gun into the bathroom. I closed my eyes and fought the ping of shame the censure in his voice elicited.

Why did I say yes out on the back patio? He seemed angry now he had to clean his gun. No, the gun didn't cause this. He put this physical distance between us every time, his passive-aggressive reminder to warn me off getting attached.

He reappeared in the bathroom doorway and leaned his shoulder against the frame. The bathroom light highlighted the silhouette of his broad shoulders and long hair hanging loose.

"Thorne's wrong." His deep voice startled me.

I pulled the sheet up to my chin. "About what?"

"I'm not rusted."

Clearing my throat bought me a second to process what he'd said. Okay, so he'd overheard my conversation with Thorne at the hospital. Which could've been bad, but after that, he'd taught me to shoot and shared a private and intimate moment with me. Well, as private as it can be in the backyard.

"Titanium doesn't rust," he continued before I caught up to him.

"He's not talking about your dick."

"I know. Heart's titanium too."

Falcon processed things quicker than I did. He was shrewd. Probably smarter than me. "I don't get it. Your heart's not rusted?"

"Nope. Can't get rusty at something you never did."

Oh. Oh. He was going about it in an indirect way, but I understood his insinuation.

"Your heart's never loved?" I asked him quietly and carefully, trying not to pressure him to open up.

He gazed out the window at the changing night sky. "No one except my mama."

Oh God. That hurt to hear. I could only imagine how it felt for him to admit it out loud. A life without love would be meaningless.

"Tried to find her."

My throat constricted. My mom. "I know."

"One man against an army down there."

"Come here."

He shook his head.

"Come back to bed. I can't stand to watch you over there anymore. Come here and let me touch you."

He paced to the bed with his head down. When he reached me, I pulled his face to mine and planted a kiss on him. "Thank you for sharing that with me. I know it's hard."

He climbed into the bed, lay on his side, and faced me. His hand reached for my hip, and he stared into my eyes. "I needed training. That's why I became a sniper. With the right motivation, you become freakishly accurate."

"I saw on the news when Guillermo joined forces with Manuel."

"I thought you didn't like to face your past."

"I didn't. Still don't. It's hard to talk about. But late at night, when I couldn't sleep, I'd look things up. See who had died, flare ups, who'd gotten arrested."

"Were you looking for me?"

"Possibly. I think so. The fifteen-year-old girl inside me always had hope you were out there fighting for us and looking for my mom."

His hand skimmed up my side and back down again. "I was, mi paloma. Anytime I got leave, I'd head down and do my surveillance. Look for her. See who was getting too powerful. Took them out. Manuel was the hardest to get alone. Ended up tricking Torrez into bringing him out in the open. Rogan and Dallas helped me take him down."

"Oh, well. That was nice of them."

"I've helped them out many times. Dallas at his wedding, Rogan with Tessa. They owed me."

"And now they're helping you with Ivan?"

"Yeah."

"You need to let me in on the planning."

"No."

"C'mon. I already know the plan. You're going to poison him."

"Jesus, woman. Don't talk about it."

"No one can hear us. At least tell me when."

He growled. "We'll leave right after your concert in New York."

"Leave for Veranistaad?"

"Yeah."

"But the sting is set for two days later."

"We'll be back before they drop dead."

"That quick?"

"In and out. Alibis on both ends. A concert then a sting. No one will notice us missing or be able to piece together a reasonable timeline for us to travel and return that fast."

"Wow. So no guns?"

"Oh, we'll be fully armed under our robes. We'll pose as Saudis. Something goes south, it'll be carnage and escape."

Oh my. He sounded so confident. "Hmm. Well, I'm terrified."

"You'll be safe here. Got a guy named Helix to watch you."

"Not scared for myself."

His hand wrapped around my neck, and his face drew closer to mine. "You're scared for me?"

"I like your titanium heart."

"And dick."

"Yes, but if you die, I'll miss your heart."

His hand squeezed my neck. "You'll miss my heart?"

"You might think you haven't loved, but you have. The years you stood by Rogan? That's love. Risking your life to fight for your country? That's love. Searching forever to find my mother. That's love."

"That's just doing what's right."

"It comes from love. And one more you need to acknowledge. Rescuing me and Soledad? Paying for our educations and expenses so we could make better lives for ourselves? That's love."

His shoulders tightened as I told him I knew his secret. "Call it what you want, it's what I do."

"It's love. You have an experienced heart. Shines like polished metal." I placed my palm flat on his left pec, feeling his warmth and heart beat against my fingertips.

"You're crazy." He tried to dismiss me, but we both knew I was on the right track.

"And the first woman you love with that heart will receive a tremendously invaluable gift."

He tucked his head into my neck and kissed my shoulder. "I won't die," he said against my skin.

I tugged his head up by the ears and forced him to look in my eyes. "Promise?"

"My promise doesn't mean much to you."

Ouch. In all my bitterness, I never stopped to think that Falcon might feel bad for failing me.

"You couldn't keep your promise. I forgive you. I know she's probably dead." My voice cracked.

"Jesus, babe. I'm sorry." He wrapped his arms around my back and pulled me into his powerful embrace.

"It's okay." Tears stung behind my eyes. My inner fifteen-year-old clung to Falcon like he could make it untrue, but I had to learn to face reality. Sometimes we lose people we love.

"Lost my mom too. Also at Manuel's hands."

Oh God, Falcon was finally opening up and sharing honestly with me. "I know."

"He's negotiating his last deal down under with the devil. He's got a choice of a burning cell or a scalding cauldron."

"Yeah." I nodded with my head on his chest.

"And our mothers are up in heaven looking down on us together in this bed," he said.

"Yeah." I giggled. "Hopefully they weren't watching earlier with the gun."

My head bobbled as he chuckled. "Nah. They cover their ears for that."

"Probably."

After a few quiet minutes, he spoke again in a quiet murmur. "The chances of me not coming back are slim. The falcon flies above the fray."

I appreciated him trying to reassure me, but this mission was extremely dangerous, and I wouldn't feel comfortable until it was over. "I hope so."

"We're the best in the world. Alpha Squadron doesn't fail. Okay not true, we've had some serious fuckups over the years, but we haven't lost a man yet. Shrapnel wounds and broken bones, yes, but we're all still breathing and fighting."

"Are Diesel and Blaze Alpha Squadron?"

"Yeah. Torrez is taking Diesel's place. He's a retired SEAL. Not part of Alpha Squadron, but Torrez wants Ivan as bad as I do. Fucker killed a lot of people and hurt a lot of women. He's been scaring you. Shot one of my men. He's history."

"Just be careful."

"Never. Always balls to the wall."

I laughed. "Okay. Well, do whatever works to keep you alive and get you back here."

"I can promise that."

Chapter 24

FALCON

"Door check," I whispered to the team via the communications headset.

Blaze, Diesel, and I were stationed to the right of the stage at The Met guarding Aida, Gaspar, and Matteo.

"Secure on one," Dallas replied.

Helix, Oz, Ruger, and two other guards from Dallas's team responded in the same fashion. We were sealed in tight.

The lights went down, the audience quieted, and the orchestra played an entrance song for Gaspar as he walked onto the stage. The roaring applause from the crowd made Aida smile but grated on my nerves.

Tickets to Gaspar's return to The Met had sold out in seconds, but security here always posed a challenge. The Met refused to allow wanding of patrons as they came in, and they limited our access backstage before the show. Even Gaspar couldn't get them to budge on those two weaknesses.

The fact a jet waited for us at JFK made us all edgy. Within twelve hours, we'd be meeting with King Ivan Sharshinbaev and slipping him the drink that would end his reign.

Tessa, Soraya, and Cecelia watched the show from their second-row seats. Rogan and Zook flanked them. Torrez sat in the front row. None of the guys had their eyes on the stage or the women. We were all on high-alert, amped up for Aida's first public performance since the last shooting.

The plan was to get the women together in the dressing room after the concert, hand them over to Dallas, Helix, and a team who would guard them at a safe house in upstate New York until we returned. Helix had returned my Sig to me, so I had two weapons tonight.

Gaspar sang his first song and took a bow. Everything was flowing smoothly.

He called Aida out on stage, and she made her grand entrance to the music of her signature aria from the opera. They embraced and she smiled at him as she spoke into the microphone.

"I can't tell you how happy I am to be back at the wonderful Metropolitan Opera with my beloved father figure, Gaspar Evaristo. After a horrible accident threatened to take his life, I thought I'd never return, not if he didn't. You'd think I would know sadness living Aida's life on the stage, but I promise you, there's no greater despair than watching a man you worship and adore fight for his life in a hospital bed."

Blaze, standing next to me, fidgeted his feet and cleared his throat as he glanced at the bandage on Diesel's head. Diesel gave him a glare. Idiots. Maybe this fucking time they'd get on with it.

Aida continued, "Gaspar Evaristo is God's precious gift to art. He shines as a beacon of light in the dark night, and he lives as an example to us all of valor and benevolence. Tonight our music will be a tribute to the beauty his life has brought to this world."

Gaspar, near tears, kissed her cheeks and beamed at her. They sang a duet of her signature aria from Aida, and the crowd loved it.

The spotlight narrowed in on her lone form against a dark cavernous stage as Gaspar took his place in the conductor's podium in front of the orchestra. Her royal purple gown glinted in the lights. It pushed up her boobs and flared out from her hips like a quinceañera gown.

Her face transformed into fifteen-year-old Magdalena. Vulnerable, insecure, and soft-spoken.

"Life isn't fair. Who lives or dies is out of our control. Fate can come at anytime and take innocent lives. This song is for the young women who lost their lives in St. Amalie." She raised a finger to her nose and sniffled. "For all the women out there who have had their future stolen from them, including my mother, and the heartbroken doves who wait in vain for their return."

Gaspar raised his baton, and the orchestra played the introductory strains to "Cucurrucucu Paloma."

She opened her mouth, and it happened again. Her voice seared my skin and woke up long-dead receptors. Art never moved me, but Aida's voice reached down and grabbed me by the balls, forcing me to feel it. It wasn't just her voice. It was her face and the way her body became a pillar of raw emotion. Everything I rejected, she embraced and made it grand.

When the crowd settled from the applause, she looked back at me for reassurance. No movement in the audience or house so things were going well. I gave her a nod to continue.

"This next song says love is letting go. This is hard because we want to hold onto what we love and letting go hurts. But... because I love him, I'm letting Thorne go." The audience murmured, and I scanned the crowd. If someone wanted to make a move, the break in the flow she created would be the ideal time. She raised her hand, palm up and waved it over to Thorne next to me. "Goodbye. I love you," she said with her eyes on Thorne. She pressed her fingers to her lips and blew him a kiss.

I stepped closer to Thorne. "What the hell was that?"

"Divorce came through today. She signed it before the show," he whispered.

She divorced him and announced it publicly? Leave it to Aida to do it with a flourish.

Holy fuck.

She was free.

Matteo joined Aida on the stage, and they belted out "Perhaps Love" with fiery adoration in their eyes, but I knew she sang every note for me.

All kinds of possibilities flooded my mind, but no time for that shit. I always kept vigilant. Many years of fuckups had taught me one truth. The second you drop your guard, you're fucked.

"Bravo!" The standing crowd shouted and cheered. Gaspar returned to the stage and took a final bow in the arms of Aida and Matteo. Thank fuck this event was coming to an end with no incidents.

Aida's eyes found mine. She dipped a deep curtsey in my direction and gave me a glowing smile. I nodded back.

Good job, mi paloma. You have bewitched us all again.

My nerves eased as the audience left the venue. Blaze, Diesel, and I guided her, Matteo, Gaspar, and Thorne to the dressing room we had secured earlier. I cleared the room and allowed everyone to enter.

Torrez, Rogan, and Zook came in behind us with Soraya, Tessa, and Cecelia.

The women huddled around Aida. The guys stayed by the door.

"You were fantastic," Tessa said. "I had goosebumps."

"How did you learn to sing like that?" Cecelia asked her.

"Many years of practice," she answered humbly, but she had a God-given talent all the practice in the world could not imitate.

"I absolutely loved it and I don't even like opera," Soraya said.

"Good. I'm glad."

I turned to Rogan. "I'll stay here. Everyone else on halls and perimeter until the venue is empty."

He nodded and the guys fanned out.

Blaze came up to me with a smarmy grin on his face. "You got a backup weapon?"

"You feel the need to be up in my business?" I returned.

"Just saying, in case your side arm gets uh," he glanced at Aida, "wet."

Fucking Blaze. Probably watched us on the video feed. "Bro code, man. You cut the feed when the action starts."

He pulled his teeth over his lower lip like a teenager who just saw his first titty flick. "Enjoyed it. Can't pay for porn like that."

Asshole. "I have two weapons. Get the fuck out of here."

"That's good. Not letting you borrow mine. Ever." He waggled his eyebrows, thinking he was smart.

"Your gun could end up in Diesel's ass any moment now. Not touching nothing of yours."

Burn. His face turned red and he stuttered. I got him. "Go guard the fucking hall and make sure the place is empty."

He gave me a smartass salute and smiled at Aida and the girls.

I closed the door and watched them chat. Aida spoke with her hands and the women laughed. They looked like fast friends already. I could see on her face she loved being the shining center of attention and a chance to make new friends.

Rogan's knock sounded at the door. His voice followed in my ear. "We got company."

I opened it to see my father standing there with a bouquet of red roses in his hands. He raised the flowers. "For the señorita."

The girls stopped talking and stared at us in the doorway.

"Told you never come near her." I spoke in Spanish to my father. Behind him, Rogan patted him down and removed his gun. He handed it to me, and I tucked it in my belt.

My father allowed all this with a calm demeanor.

"You may take my gun, Primitivo. She's the closest thing to a daughter I've ever known."

Goddamn asshole took the money and went back on his word. I should've known better than to make a deal with the devil. "She's not your daughter and not interested in a relationship with you. So get out."

I felt Aida approach behind me. "What is it, Falcon?" she asked in English.

"My father wishes to speak with Magdalena Esperanza," I responded in English so everyone in the room could be a witness if something went down.

"I am not her." Aida lied.

"I can see you are her as sure as Claudia were standing here in front of me," my father said with longing in his eyes for her.

"I don't know anyone named Claudia."

"If you were Magdalena, and I'm sure you are and deceiving me, I would simply ask that we could be a family. I loved your mother. Manuel took her from me, but I've missed her for many years."

Aida stared at him, confused. My father was a master manipulator. His plea now confused me too. But I wasn't stupid. He could never earn my trust.

"That's unfortunate, but you have the wrong person." Aida's continued lie to him told me she didn't trust him either.

"Fine. Then, Aida..." My father bowed to her. "Allow me to give you these roses. Your performance tonight was magical."

I took the roses and handed them to Rogan. "Trash these."

My father frowned at the lost flowers but continued to talk to Aida, "I am Guillermo de la Cruz. Primitivo's father. Surely you recognize me."

"I don't, but it's nice to meet you, Mr. de la Cruz. If you don't mind, my friends and I are having a private celebration and..."

I didn't hear the rest of Aida's sentence because a shot rang out in my earpiece. Helix's urgent voice came through the comms. "He got past me. He's coming your way. Be ready."

As Helix spoke, Rogan and I made eye contact. We pushed the girls, Gaspar, Soledad, Matteo, and Thorne to the bathroom we had converted into a safe room.

"Active shooter." Helix's frantic voice and running footsteps came through in my ear piece. More shots. "Shit. More than one. Need backup here on the south side of the building. There could be more on the other side. Who's over there?"

"This is Dallas on the south side. I don't see anyone."

"They're running into the storage area. Need backup. I'm going in."

Another gunshot drew screams from the women. Zook and Torrez had drawn their weapons and stood guard at the open door of the safe room. "Zook, you stay with them. Nobody but me. Open this for no one but me."

He nodded, holding his gun ready. He looked scared too, but in control.

"Who is that, Primitivo? Who is shooting?" my father asked.

Before I closed the door, Aida screamed, "Those are the men who killed my mother!"

"We don't know who it is," I snapped at her.

"Give me my weapon, Primitivo." My father held out his hand.

"No." As if I would give Satan a weapon in the middle of a gun fight.

"If they killed Claudia, they are my enemy too. I'll help you. We fight together again."

Fuck it. To save time, I handed him the weapon. "Get away from Aida and stay in front of me." Let him betray me, give me cause to kill him. A test under pressure.

He nodded, took the weapon, and moved to the door. I stayed close behind him, prepared for him to make a move. He didn't. He took measured steps into the hallway with his gun drawn, ready to fight by my side. Maybe my father wasn't lying. Maybe he really wanted to make amends. I'd have to think about that later because automatic fire echoed through the corridor and people were running and screaming to get away.

As Rogan and I braced, my father turned and aimed his weapon at me.

I nailed him in the neck with a roundhouse kick before he could get a shot off. He grunted as I yanked his arms behind his back, threw him to the ground, and tied his hands with a zip tie.

"You fucking mother fucker. Betray me while I'm taking fire."

He didn't reply or fight the restraints.

"We gotta go." Rogan kept his aim down the hallway. "Leave him."

"At least three shooters. Where the fuck are you guys?" Helix called over the comms.

"Torrez and Blaze are on their way. They're not there yet?" I replied.

"Okay shit. I see them."

"We're coming too. Where are you?"

"South entrance to the set storage area." We ran through the corridor in the direction of the shots. We reached the storage area and spread out along the walls.

All the actors and staff had evacuated the backstage area. A long silence passed with no shots. My heart pounded loudly in my chest.

I grabbed a chair and tossed it to the middle of the room. The shooter revealed his location when he shot at it, and Rogan shot him. A guy in a suit fell. He could be Russian, but hard to tell.

I took point down the hall, Rogan at my six. We moved slowly, listening for any movement. We heard running and heavy breathing in the comms, but no shots.

Where the fuck were the other shooters?

We turned a corner and there. Hiding behind the stage, another guy in a tux, crouched down. He got several shots off aimed at us. I unloaded four bullets into him and he collapsed. "Two down," Rogan called.

The gunfire through the comms ceased.

"Got one more here," Helix replied.

"Did you see more than three?" Rogan asked.

"I saw three," Helix replied.

"Clear it," Rogan called in the comms. If there were only three, we got them all.

"Open the door!" My father's yell came from back in the dressing room where we'd left the women.

I snagged the shooter's weapon from his dying body and stalked back to the hallway where I'd left my father. There was nothing there. Where did he go?

"Open the door!" My father's voice again.

"Get away from the fucking door, or I'll shoot you through it." Zook's voice. He was bluffing. I'd told him the door was bulletproof.

I found my father on the floor in front of the door. "Lena, she's not dead. I will bring you to her, just please, open the door."

He was lying to her to save his damn life. "Don't open the door, Zook," I said.

"Not," his muffled voice answered back.

My dad rolled to his side, his arms tied behind his back. "Tivo." He must've scooted there on his belly like a worm. "Mercy. Please. Forgive me."

I aimed the shooter's rifle at this head. "Too late, Papá."

Six rounds hit him fast in the face and chest. Watched my father's body shake, the shock on his eyes, blood starting to pour.

It was over. No more battle. I won.

I walked the rifle back to the shooter and left it by his hand.

Rogan was the only one who saw me. "Shooter hit my father."

He hated when I did illegal shit, but he'd back me if I asked him to and I was asking. He nodded.

"Looks clear," Helix said. Dallas and the other guys all responded with *clear* as they checked through the opera house.

Torrez came running into the room. "Everyone okay?"

I dragged my father's body out of the way so Aida wouldn't have to step over him. "Let's get them out."

We opened the door to a group of terrified people hunched in the corner.

"It's okay now," I said.

Aida ran into my arms and cried. "What happened?"

"We'll talk later. Need to get you out of the building first."

Sirens approached.

Aida gasped when she saw my father's body.

"Shooter got him. There's lots of bodies. Don't look."

NYPD showed up. "Hands up. Police."

I raised my hands but blocked Aida. "We're security. We neutralized the threat."

"I don't give a fuck who you are. Keep your hands up until we disarm you and clear the building."

"We cleared the fucking building."

We had a long night ahead of us explaining this shit to the authorities.

Guess we'd be late for our flight to Veranistaad, but nothing would deter us. Ivan would be the next to die.

Chapter 25

———

AIDA

Falcon refused to cancel the trip to Veranistaad.

I refused to give up on the sting operation.

After a lot of fighting that ended in angry sex, we agreed to reschedule everything as soon as possible. They wanted to get to Ivan before he heard the news of the dead hitmen at the Met gala.

Falcon and Alpha Squadron left New York after two grueling days of interrogations by the NYPD, FBI, and the CIA. We had agreed to keep the sting and plans to murder Ivan secret. The questioning was tough, but I'd held firm.

While they were gone, Isabella and Thorne helped me move all the planned escort meetings from last night to tomorrow night. It kept my mind off the insane danger of their mission.

They'd returned late in the afternoon today. Falcon only said everything was "fine" and I didn't ask the details. I was so happy he'd made it back safely, I jumped him and we spent the rest of the day in bed.

Now I was pissed because Falcon chose the absolute wrong moment to "inform" me I would be directing the sting from Boston, where we had a smaller group of women scheduled, instead of New York, where more of the action would happen.

"I'm not going to Boston," I said again.

His arm tightened around my waist as he held me from behind. "You fucking are," he growled in my ear.

"I have twice as many meet ups scheduled here in the city."

"And that's why you're going to Boston."

"Ivan is dead. Your father is dead. There is no one left to kill me."

Falcon pushed up out of the bed, which he knew bothered me. He knew I liked it when he stayed. "No one except a bunch of angry pimps who just had their cash flow cut off because Ivan dropped dead."

"I can stay at the shelter in New York."

"You will stay at the hotel in Boston." He pulled up his jeans, which he also knew I hated. It created distance between us.

I stood up and held the sheet in front of me. He glared at it. He didn't like barriers either. "Gah! You are so frustrating!"

He swooped an arm behind my back and mashed my boobs against his chest. "If you had a girl you loved, would you plop her down in the middle of a sting in New York City?"

I opened my mouth to fight back but... "A girl I loved?"

He tilted his head to the side. "Okay, a guy you loved."

A guy I loved? "Um, I would absolutely plop you down in the middle of a sting in New York City. You're the best person to be there."

He stared at me and blinked. "You saying you love me?"

"Are you saying you love me?" I asked back.

He spun us and dropped to the bed, pulling me down on top of him. I managed to keep the sheet over my front, but my back was exposed. "Are you asking me if I love you?" His deep voice rasped.

"I'm not going to Boston." I tried to change the topic.

He sat up and adjusted my legs until I straddled him. I wasn't done fighting yet, but his big hot body made my stomach flutter so I stayed put. He grinned up at me. "We're not talking about that anymore. We're talking about love."

I shook my head. "That's not something you talk about."

"No, but you do. And since it's important to you, it's something I wanna talk about too."

"Okay."

His face softened and his eyes warmed, but he didn't say anything.

"And?"

He looked down between my legs and tugged my hips forward with a soft grunt. His eyes grew hot as he watched my naked sex, covered by only a thin sheet, slide over his hard cock in his jeans. A tremor rumbled through my core as I let him rub me how he wanted. He brought a hand up to my neck and pulled me in for a kiss. It was sublime. I broke the kiss.

His hand kept pressure on my neck, so I spoke close to his lips. "This is not talking."

"Oh, we're talking."

"With words, Falc. We're having a fight and talking about love. Not making out." I pulled free of his grasp and sat up straighter.

"We're not having a fight. You're going to Boston, or we're going back to handcuffed to the bed. Not optional. Not metaphorical."

I growled at him. "You would really handcuff me to the bed while you go out and execute my sting operation?"

His eyebrows drew together. "Whoa. Your sting?"

"Yes. I did all the work."

He chuckled and looked down. "You helped, babe. You did good finding the girls, but we did all the work. We are the ones who are gonna approach, convince the girls to leave with us, and get them out safely."

I stared at him through narrowed eyes. He really thought he had the harder job here? "And I'm the one who will have a huge team of women waiting to help them. I am the one who'll face their tears, suffer with them as they accept what's happened, and cry with them when they realize all they've lost and could regain."

He chewed his lip and his big warm hands caressed up and down my thighs. "You're right. You have the harder job. I could not handle all that."

"Exactly. I can and I have many times."

He nodded and pulled me in for a wet kiss. Did I win? It felt like I won that one.

He ended the kiss and his gaze bore into mine. "I sit you down on my lap like this and tell you I want you to do something that will keep you safe, I'm telling you I love you."

My heart jumped into my throat.

"First and only woman I'll ever love."

My lips pressed together, an ugly cry brewing. Falcon talking so openly melted my heart.

"You saying no, you want to take a risk I'm not comfortable with, that's like saying no to letting me love you. That's the way I'm gonna show it. By keeping your safety in mind in everything we do."

He looked so completely vulnerable and sexy, telling me he loved me in his own special way.

"Now, do you love me, mi paloma?" The corner of his mouth quirked up.

I nodded. "I do."

He took that in then said, "Then you come to Boston with me tomorrow and run the operation from the base there. Get your girls to cover you here, but you'll be with me in Boston." He squeezed my thighs. "Because I love you."

Engage full on ugly cry. No holding it back. Big wet crocodile tears dripped from my eyes. "I love you too, Falcon."

"Good."

Chapter 26

FALCON GAVE THE STING and set up the same careful attention he gave to everything. He reserved extra hotel rooms in Boston in case we needed the space and installed the doors, cameras, and alarms he always used for my rooms.

I had helped him and his team arrange forty meetings with escorts with possible connections to Ivan's ring. Dallas trained and provided eighty men for the night.

The setups in New York and Atlanta were double this size. If all went well, we'd have as many as two hundred victims rescued tonight. If we didn't get shut down by the authorities, we'd plan another sting of the same size in the Midwest and one more on the West Coast.

I gasped when I first saw Falcon's disguise. He'd let his beard get scraggly and untamed for his trip to Veranistad. He wore a stretched-out double extra large threadbare tee under a tattered old flannel. His jeans looked like rejects from the eighties and had mud stains on the knees. His hair was dull and tied in a bun instead of hanging loose or a ponytail and his eyes were brown. My commando defender with big muscles had transformed into the construction worker down the street. A guy you might see drinking at a bar downtown.

"Wow. You look absolutely ordinary."

"Well, thank you."

"How did you do that?"

"Told you I'd worn a lot of uniforms. When blending in is important, I can do that."

I patted his chest and felt the iron strength hidden under his loose clothes. "This is perfect. You won't scare the women, and they'll be able to trust you."

"Yeah." He scanned the conference room full of people.

Fifty women who had been rescued by me waited as volunteers to help with the intake and transition of the victims. Isabella ran up to me and gave me a warm hug.

"How are you, darling?" I kissed her cheek.

She smelled like flowers, her hair shone bright, and she wore a beautiful navy-blue dress. "I was doing good, Aida. Holding down a job. Then Sergio found me." She lowered her head.

Oh no. Her old pimp. "Did he hurt you?"

"No. He said he's disappointed in me. Wants me back in his stable."

"You talked to him?" I looked up to see concern in Falcon's eyes. His agreement to all this had been tentative, knowing we'd piss off a lot of pimps by convincing their girls to leave.

"He's not a bad guy. I mean, I left him hanging with one less girl," Isabella said.

Oh my God, the number these guys did on these women. "That is not on you. It's on him."

"He's worried I'm going to turn him in to the cops, but I told him I wouldn't."

Oh lordy. This was not good. "Don't talk to him again, and if he comes near you, call me or Falcon right away."

She nodded. "Okay."

"I'll check in with you tomorrow." We had to start tonight's activities or the guys would miss their appointments. "Thank you for being here to help. It's going to be difficult and rewarding, I hope."

"I'm so excited to be part of this." The smile returned to her beautiful face.

"Why don't you ask everyone to take a seat so we can go over the plan for tonight? Pass these out for me, will you?"

"Of course." She took the stack of papers with scripts and procedures in both English and Spanish and handed them out to everyone.

I stopped when I saw Torrez and Soraya, Rogan and Tessa, Zook and Cecelia, Dallas and Cyan, Diesel and Blaze, and Thorne and Matteo enter the room. The guys all wore loose-fitting casual clothes, like Falcon had worn. Except Blaze, who had his hair combed forward like a geek. He wore big turtle-rimmed glasses and a cheesy buttoned up Polo shirt and high-belted pants. Oh, how funny. It worked though.

Guys like that often sought to pay for sex. They were usually a lot smaller and less gorgeous, but his disguise would suit our purposes.

"This is a surprise!" I opened my arms and received warm hugs from the women.

"We wanted to be here with you tonight." Soraya spoke for the group.

"I know, but don't you guys have to get going?" I asked Rogan.

"We have some time," Rogan responded as he glanced at his watch.

"Alright. Take a seat. We're going to start soon."

As they joined the group, Falcon leaned down to whisper in my ear, "You're on, babe." He kissed my cheek and backed away. He stood behind me in the doorway.

"Hello, everyone. Thank you so much for being here. Tonight isn't going to be easy. In a few hours, broken women will walk through that door." I looked back at Falcon watching me and my heart warmed. *He loves me.* "Their choices and dignity have been stripped from them. They've been violated and brainwashed. Seeing them will open old wounds and you will cry." Tessa, Soraya, Cecelia, and half the women in the audience were already wiping at their eyes. "If you don't cry, you're stronger than me. There will be pain and healing, for all of us. Always be patient. Expect every woman you encounter to be terrified for her safety for betraying her pimp. She may lash out at you. She won't trust you, but she will remember every word you say. It may be the first kind words she's heard from anyone in years." Well, shoot. I had to stop and wipe my eye. I chuckled inside at my own weakness. "Please use the script we handed out. We've found that these are the words that will get the best response. *You are safe. I know you feel scared because I have been where you are. My name is Aida, and I'm here for you.*"

I took a deep breath to gather myself. This was so hard, but we had to be strong.

"You are safe." A sweet voice came at me from the door, interrupting my speech. I didn't turn around. My stomach fluttered. The voice continued, "I know you must be scared. I've been where you are. My name is Claudia, and I'm here for you."

Not one muscle in my body moved. That voice took me back. I was fifteen again. I was scared and hiding next to Primitivo's truck as bullets exploded inside my home. My heart was torn from my body as I boarded a boat without her. My soul slowly shriveled as I realized Tivo would never return with her. And finally, just a few days ago, in front of Primitivo's father, I mourned as I accepted her death.

But now. Now, her voice called to me. A mother to a daughter.

I'm here for you.

Could she be here? I only needed to turn around to see. My hands trembled. My breath came hard and shallow. Falcon's warm touch on my back woke me from my stupor. I looked up at him. "Is it really her?"

He nodded. "Turn around, mi paloma."

His hands on my shoulders forced me to pivot. I closed my eyes and when I opened them. I saw her.

My mother.

Her eyebrows crunched in worry. She looked older. Her hair gray, but lord almighty, my mother was standing in the doorway, her arms halfway up, waiting for me to accept her.

I was fifteen and lost. Confused. My own eyes stared back at me in her face.

Falcon's warm breath hit my ear. "Go to her, babe." The pads of his fingers pressed to my back. His light touch propelled me like I was on ice skates in a vacuum.

I made it to my mom and embraced her. "Mama?"

"Magdalena." She made a sharp sound stuck between a laugh and sob. "I have missed you so."

"Mama?" I pulled back to touch her face with shaking hands. I couldn't see through the deluge of tears. A nervous laugh escaped my throat. "It's really you?"

"Yes, yes, dear. I'm here and I love you." Her smile turned down into a grimace of pain.

"No." My head fell to her shoulder, and I let the tears stream down. She wept into my shoulder, her hands around me, her arms pulling me close. She smelled good. Unfamiliar yet also exactly like my mom. My fifteen-year-old self hugged her and absorbed her warmth. My mother was alive. And slowly, as we embraced and cried, I grew up. My withered fifteen-year-old soul came to life and bloomed into a thirty-seven year old woman about to explode with love.

"I love you, Mama. I love you."

"Yes. It's okay, my Lena. I love you. We're back together now. No one will separate us again."

We stayed like that for a long time, only the two of us locked in an embrace. A sniffle and a cough caused me to stir. She squeezed my elbow and lifted her head. Her eyes glanced to Falcon and the crowd I had completely forgotten.

"Oh, um." I turned to face them with my arm around her waist. "This is my mom."

Teary eyed women clapped for us. The men didn't cry, but the emotion coming off of them filled the room. This sent me into more tears. Falcon put an arm over my shoulders and dropped a reassuring kiss on my temple. "Isabella, can you take over for Aida?"

"Sure. Of course." She came up and hugged me. "Congratulations. I wish I could find my mother too."

"Yes. I know."

"Let's go over here and talk," Falcon said. "Isabella will carry on for you." He guided us both over to a table in the corner. I did not let go of my mother's hands. They felt fragile and wrinkled, but she looked incredible. She had a simple gold band on her left finger. "Are you married?"

"Yes. I have a husband and three half-siblings for you to meet. Not tonight. I flew in alone. It was sudden. As soon as I heard Guillermo was dead, I came to you right away."

"You knew where I was?"

"Not until recently. I saw you in the news when you won the award."

"You didn't contact me?"

"No. I'm so sorry. I was scared of Guillermo and Manuel."

"I understand."

"No. It's not forgivable. I should've sought you out sooner."

"It's okay."

"I thought they were targeting you," she whispered.

"No. Ivan," I replied. We couldn't really speak freely here.

"Yes. I know that now. Falcon found me and told me they were all dead."

I smiled at him. "You found her? How?

"After you won the Latina Choice Award, she started following you online."

"Lots of people follow me online."

"Diesel and I went through all of them, narrowed them down to women your mom's age, and contacted them."

"You contacted all the women my mom's age who follow me?"

"Yes."

"That must've taken forever."

"Patience and persistence. She filtered up to the top because she checked your website several times a day."

I looked back at my mom. "You checked my website?"

"All day long. I wanted to hear everything about you."

"I'm sorry for everything." I squeezed her hands. "I looked for you for many years. Falcon did too."

Her mouth turned down in a frown. "I looked for you too."

"Where were you?" I asked her.

"Manuel sold me to one of Ivan's handlers. My husband helped me escape. We moved to California."

"You were in California? I'm there all the time," I said. So close.

"We could have crossed paths," she said with bitter regret.

I touched her face. "Well, now we're together."

"Yes." She smiled. "Now, from what I understand, you have an elaborate rescue operation planned tonight."

I nodded.

She patted my hands. "Let's get to work. I'm here to help."

I grabbed Falcon's face and pulled him in for a kiss. "Thank you."

He smiled. "Sorry it's late."

"You're amazing. It happened as it was meant to be."

"I'm happy for you," he whispered in my ear.

"I love you so much right now," I whispered back.

"Same, mi paloma. Same."

I stared into his staggeringly beautiful eyes. How could one man be so gorgeous and sexy and sweet all in one fabulous package?

"We need to get going," he said as he glanced toward the guys gathering by the exit. He made eye contact with Helix, who would stay with me tonight.

"Please be careful," I said.

"Be ready. When Alpha Squadron has a mission, we come through."

"We'll be ready."

I kissed him goodbye and watched him walk over to Rogan and the guys, who had already kissed their wives goodbye. They headed out the door casually. This was easy work for them.

Chapter 27

FALCON

We gathered in the lobby for a last-minute briefing. I was going over the procedure when Lachlan Cutlass walked through the hotel main entrance with another dude.

What the fuck was he doing here? Last thing we needed was the FBI involved in this.

Rogan greeted him with a chin tilt and we formed a small group away from the other men. "What're you doing here, Cutlass?"

"FBI wants in on your op," he replied.

"There is no op," Rogan lied.

"No bullshit, Rogan. We know what you've planned and we want the pimps."

"Who's this guy?" Rogan asked about the other guy he came in with.

"This is Detective Colt Lacy. Boston PD." Lachlan aimed his thumb at his friend.

Rogan looked to the ceiling. "Fuck. No. No feds, no cops. We're just talking to a few girls, trying to convince them to start fresh. Nothing for you to see here."

"We want the pimps," the detective repeated Lachlan's idea.

"We get the cops involved, this whole op goes belly up," I said. "The girls get arrested, they get scared, we lose them. Not the purpose of this mission." We knew the feds would probably be watching us tonight, but we'd bet on them not interfering. Chance we took.

"You guys have penetrated deep into a ring we've been working for a long time. You get the girls to turn and testify, we don't prosecute them for prostitution, and they get witness protection if they want it." Lachlan laid a tempting card on the table.

Rogan looked to me for an answer. I raised my eyebrows. It wasn't a bad idea. I wanted the pimps too. Getting the girls out always seemed weak to me, but the best we could do without the authorities on our side.

"If we get a deal going with the feds, we could make a much bigger impact," I said to Rogan.

He narrowed his eyes at Lachlan. "The feds giving away Wit Sec now for hookers? Not high profile enough."

"It's privately funded. A bunch of celebrities set up the funding for a protection agency for sex trade workers. The girls will get first-class treatment, counseling, identity relocation if they ask for it." He grinned because he knew he had a rock-solid offer.

Everything he said lined up with the goals of Aida's organization. It would take some of the funding pressure off Torrez and Dallas. Shit. If we took it far enough, Dallas might enter into an agreement with the FBI and get them off his back. Might work out. Could also fail horribly.

"We'll give it a shot," Rogan said. "You let tonight go down as planned. We'll give you access to the women tomorrow. Tonight, no cops. The volunteers get the intake done. You show up tomorrow and ask them to turn on the pimps. Do not scare them into running back."

Colt nodded. "We can do that."

"We gotta get going," I said. Rogan and I needed to discuss this alone.

"Good luck, guys." Lachlan gave Rogan a thumbs up and left with his friend.

Rogan looked skeptically at Lachlan's back.

"Blow it off, Rogan. Let's get this thing done."

Not one to waste time, Rogan returned to the group and picked up where he'd left off.

I ENTERED THE HOTEL room for my nine pm appointment. The girl hid behind the door and peeked one eye around.

"Hello, honey." Her voice sounded scratchy.

I sat in a chair. "You comin' out?"

She closed the door and I saw her for the first time. Pink mini skirt and tank top. Skinny. No hips. Flat ass. Lips all wrong. Clearly a dude.

"What'll it be?" she asked.

If I called her out for being a man right away, I'd lose her trust.

"Just wanna talk."

She frowned and ran her hand over her wig. "You want me to suck your dick? Unless you want ass. You seem like the kinda guy who likes ass."

Holy shit. How did I end up in this situation? "Relax, turbo. I'm not here for sex."

"You're not? Are you a cop?"

"Nope. Here to talk to you."

Twenty minutes later, she'd taken off her wig and admitted to being male cross-dresser. I talked to him about leaving his pimp. He resisted at first, but the promise of witness protection threw him over the edge. He wanted out. He was just scared. I gave him the sweats and T-shirt kit and he changed his clothes.

Aida was a little surprised when I showed up with a dude wearing lipstick, but she recovered quickly and handed him over to the volunteers.

It was a helluva week with Aida. But then again, every week with her was eventful. Sure as hell not boring.

BY THE END OF THE NIGHT, the team rescued twenty-one women and one man. The volunteers helped them get settled in the hotel rooms on the top floor. Aida said a tearful goodnight to her mother, and we headed back to our suite.

I got her naked and pushed her exhausted body into the shower. I climbed in behind her and held her up as the water washed everything away.

"You did so much for me. I'm so grateful." Her words slurred, she was so tired.

"I'd do anything for you, mi paloma. Dive on a grenade for you." It was true. The woman had my loyalty now.

"No, please. Don't do that."

"Hush." I massaged shampoo into her hair and she moaned.

I wrapped her in a towel and fell in bed behind her. "Gotta tell you one thing before I let you sleep."

"Okay."

"Rogan has a contact at the FBI, Lachlan Cutlass. He's been following us."

"Uh oh."

"It's good."

"Does he suspect you killed Ivan?"

"He didn't mention it."

"Why do you bring it up?"

"He wants to talk to the women tomorrow."

"I don't want to involve the FBI."

"Right. He wants to talk to them. We don't have a lot of choices. We say no, they shut us down, arrest us all for soliciting prostitution."

"Oh."

"So, he's offering rehabilitation and protection for the girls. Similar to what you do but he has more funding."

"He does?"

"Some private celebrity charity to fight human trafficking."

"Oh. Wow. That might be awesome."

"Yeah, Rogan took the deal, with tomorrow being a test run."

"Okay."

"They have to turn and testify against the pimps."

"Oh. They might not like that, but if you offer them protection, they might be more cooperative. I like the idea."

"Let's wait and see."

"Okay."

"Sleep."

"I love you, Falcon."

I squeezed her close and kissed her neck, but didn't say anything. I let her sleep. First thing in the morning, I made slow love to her and showed her how I felt.

Chapter 28

———

TESSA DECKED OUT HER ranch house for Christmas again this year. She added stacked candles that spelled out the word *LOVE*. She was in on my covert plans for tonight, but I did not tell Rogan. Couldn't bear the ridicule.

Tessa's excitement was way more than I could stomach, but she came through in flying colors and hopefully she'd managed to keep the secret from Rogan.

We all took seats at extended tables that ran from the dining room to the living room. All the suspects from last year were here, plus Aida, Soledad and her husband, Taye. Thorne brought his brother and seemed happy. Gaspar and Marcella being there made Tessa nervous at first because she'd never had celebrities in her house before, but the large crown absorbed them and the tension passed.

Aida had quickly become close with Claudia, her husband, and their kids, who all came tonight. Plus two new arrivals from Veranistaad, Narium and Fasul. Narium had been victimized just like Cecelia and Soraya. Fasul had helped Zook when he needed it. Torrez and Zook sponsored them to come to the States after King Ivan died. They looked very happy about their first Christmas in America.

Milo, Tessa's younger brother, had grown a foot in the past year. He had his eyes on Aida all evening. "Hey, kid."

"Hi, Falcon. Did you know Aida is a rock star?"

"Yeah. Heard that."

This year Rogan didn't even ask Tessa to bring the food out first. The new tradition was cemented in stone. The food would come after the speech.

Although this year, Tessa and I had something up our sleeves.

Tessa whispered in Rogan's ear, and his gaze slid to mine. First he looked surprised, then distrustful. I raised my brows.

What, bro? You don't trust me with your speech?

He must've seen I was serious because he nodded his head.

Go ahead.

I stood up and cleared my throat. The shocked reaction from all the seated people made me chuckle. Not one person in that room expected me to stand up and talk.

"Hey. I got something to say."

The room went deathly quiet and what Aida must feel before she goes on stage zipped through me. I glanced down into her sweet eyes and found the words.

"Rogan usually makes a dumbass speech at this time."

Tessa scowled at me. Right. No cussing. Or insulting Rogan. Let me try again.

"I mean. This year I'll be making the speech before Christmas dinner."

This got me a few dropped jaws.

"Yeah, I'm as surprised as you are. But I wanted to say something in front of all of you." I downed a shot of whiskey and gritted my teeth through the burn. Tessa nodded to encourage me. "Sometimes you think you know something. Then you find out you were wrong. Alpha Squadron's been my life for a long time. Gave up everything for this group of men. In the beginning, there was just us. We spent our Christmases trying to find a flat surface to catch some sleep. But then Rogan met Tessa, and our work with the government came to an end. I'm not sure what I'm saying. I suck at this. I didn't even have falling in love on my radar before. But I smashed into this woman again and everything changed. She's a good woman. She cares about other people. She's incredibly talented, and she's more grateful than anyone here to have Christmas with you all. So I'm saying this in front of you so you see how important it is. I'm marrying her." I heard her gasp and a few awws from the girls. Nothing from the men. I was pretty sure I'd stunned them into silence.

"I told her we'd have to wait and see. I waited and I saw. I saw I was mistaken. My life was missing something. The kind of love only a good woman can fill. So this woman here and her voice convinced me. We have no solid plan. We don't know how Alpha Squadron will fit in. All I know is I'll be by her side for every song she sings and she'll be by mine for whatever the heck is in store for me. We started this journey together a long time ago. Twenty-three years ago. And we still have a lot of life left to live. Whatever time I got left, I'm gonna spend it listening to her voice, and enjoying the love she gives me."

I grabbed her hand and made her stand. Her shocked eyes made me laugh. "Aida, marry me." I held up the ring.

She mumbled something and looked around the room like, is this really happening?

"You say, *yes, Falcon, I'll marry you.*"

"Yes, Falcon." Her lips sputtered.

"*I'll marry you,*" I repeated.

"I'll marry you," she said with her mouth all twisted in emotion.

I slipped the ring on her finger and kissed her deep and hard. Cheers and jeers erupted. She whimpered when I ended the kiss. "Alright then. Show's over. We'll send you all an invitation."

Everyone laughed and we sat down. She started kissing me like crazy. I slipped a hand into her hair and deepened it.

Milo giggled.

I licked her lips and kissed her smile. "Happy?"

"Beyond happy."

"Good. Let's eat."

Chapter 29

———

AFTER DINNER, SHE DRAGGED me out to the patio where it was snowing.

"It's cold as fuck out here, babe."

"You want to get married? To me?" She sounded shocked. Was she not at the table just now?

"Definitely."

Her shoulders shook and her lip quivered. "I have a tour in Italy."

I stepped close and held her shivering body in my arms. "Then I'm going to see Italy for the first time."

"You've never seen Italy?"

"If they didn't have a war and Guillermo didn't expand his operations to Europe, I didn't have a need to go there."

"The Amalfi Coast?"

"Never even heard of it."

"Oh, Falcon. It's gorgeous." She smiled.

"Then you'll show it to me."

Her hands came up to her mouth. "Oh my God. You're going to travel with me?"

"Yes. I'm your head of security."

"Oh lordy lordy." She patted her chest with her hand, trying not to hyperventilate. The ring looked good on her finger.

"Couple conditions," I said.

"You and your conditions!"

"When we're in Los Angeles, we stay in the mansion in Beverly Hills."

Her eyes widened but she nodded. "If it's available to rent, I would love that."

"It's available. I bought it."

"You bought it?"

"You liked it and it has a kickass security setup."

She laughed. "Yes, it does."

"It's got great privacy on the patio if I decide to fuck you with my gun again, or anything else I want to do to you out there."

"Shut up."

I pulled her in closer and tried to keep her warm with my arms. "When you're in New York, we come to Boston and visit these folks. They're my family."

"Yes, yes. Of course. I love them all."

"Then we have an arrangement." I kissed her frozen nose.

"An understanding." She smiled up at me.

"A marriage," I said, making it clear I was dead serious.

"I can't believe this."

"Can I convince you to believe inside? My balls are freezing."

She jumped on her tiptoes and kissed me. Her lips were cold from the snowflakes that had melted there, but I bit her lower lip and she opened for me.

Nothing cold about Aida's mouth.

Hot as hell and all mine.

Forever.

Want More?

SIGN UP TO BEX DANE's VIP reader team and receive exclusive bonus content including;

- Free Books

- Deleted scenes

- Secrets no one else knows

- Advanced Reader Copies and first look at cover reveals

Give me more[1]!

51469577R00199

Made in the USA
Lexington, KY
03 September 2019